A Time Apart

Diane Stanley

A Time Apart

MORROW JUNIOR BOOKS

New York

Published by Morrow Junior Books
a division of William Morrow and Company, Inc.
1350 Avenue of the Americas, New York, NY 10019
www.williammorrow.com

Printed in the United States of America.

10 9 8 7 6 5 4 3 2 1

Library of Congress Cataloging-in-Publication Data
Stanley, Diane.
A time apart / by Diane Stanley.
p. cm.
Summary: While her mother undergoes treatment for cancer, thirteen-year-old
Ginny is sent to live with her father in England, where she becomes part of an
archeological experiment to investigate life during the Iron Age.
ISBN 0-688-16997-X
[1. Mothers and daughters—Fiction.   2. Fathers and daughters—Fiction.
3. Interpersonal relations—Fiction.   4. Iron age—Fiction.   5. Archaeology—
Fiction.]   I. Title.   PZ7.S7869Tg 1999   [Fic]—dc21   99-13659   CIP

In memory of
Fay Stanley Shulman
1920–1990

THE IRON AGE was a period in the process of human cultural development, coming after the Stone Age and the Bronze Age. In Europe the Iron Age began around 800 B.C., when the Celtic peoples began to replace their bronze tools with those made of a superior metal, iron. In Britain the period lasted for almost a thousand years, until the arrival of the Romans in A.D. 43 ushered in the Modern Age.

Participants in the Project

Virginia ("Ginny") Dorris—age thirteen

Hugh Dorris—Ginny's father, an anthropology professor at a London university

Tom Fielding—a doctoral candidate in English literature and an aspiring writer, father of Daisy

Liz Fielding—a graduate student in psychology, mother of Daisy

Daisy Fielding—age five

Mark Potter—a carpenter and craftsman of fine furniture

Karen Potter—a nurse

Jonas Kirkland—high school science teacher

Bunny Kirkland—elementary school teacher

Nathaniel ("Nat") Kirkland—age ten

Samuel ("Sam") Kirkland—age eight

Bennett Clark—travel agent

Faith Clark—florist

Corey Donnelley—Faith's younger brother, age seventeen

Ian Munson—auto mechanic, avid outdoorsman

Millie Munson—aerobics instructor, former marathon runner

Dr. Maurice Everett—chairman of the Anthropology Department at the university, director of the project

Chapter 1

WHEN GINNY ARRIVED at London's Gatwick Airport after an eight-hour transatlantic flight, her father was not there to meet her. She was thirteen years old, and her sole preparation for emergencies was one hundred dollars in American bills and a list of telephone numbers. She had not wanted to make this visit, much less make it by herself, but she was under the impression that her father was looking forward to it. At the very least she had expected him to show up.

She looked at the crowd gathered on the far side of the customs barrier. Some of them seemed quite excited, waving and cheering as they spotted their friends. None of their faces looked familiar. Ginny wondered, with mixed hope and dismay, whether she had merely forgotten what he looked like.

As the crowd began to thin, she noticed several people holding signs, a few of them crudely hand-lettered. One said VICTORIA TOURS and was held at chest height by a bored-looking man who gazed vacantly into the middle distance. Off to the left she spotted another man, with dark, bushy hair and protuberant eyes magnified by thick, rimless glasses. He was looking straight at her in a curious, froglike way. He was holding a sign too, and it had her name on it.

She headed in his direction, trailing her little black suitcase. "I'm Virginia Dorris," she said.

The young man smiled and took her bag, introduced himself as Roger, and explained that he had been sent to pick her up by someone named Maurice. This worried Ginny because she had no idea who that was.

"I was supposed to meet my dad," she said.

Roger continued smiling; it seemed to be his one expression. "Your dad couldn't get away," he said. "Maurice said he'd take you out there. This way!" Confident that she would follow, he strode off toward the exit. After all, he had her suitcase.

"But I don't know him—Maurice," Ginny insisted, trotting alongside Roger as he briskly wove his way through gaps in the crowd, expertly steering around cartloads of luggage.

"Dr. Everett," he called over his shoulder. "Maurice Everett." When Ginny still showed no sign of understanding, he added, "Head of the department—you know?— your dad's boss."

"Oh," said Ginny. She had never heard his name before. That would be the man who had designed the Iron Age project from which her father "couldn't get away."

"I'm just going to be there for a little while," she said.

Back home in Houston her mother would be asleep. Ginny pictured her curled up under her beautiful Nantucket quilt, with its soft fabric and faded colors.

Then she realized with a pang that her mom might not be at home, after all, but at the hospital. Was the surgery today or would it be tomorrow? Why hadn't she gotten all that straight? There had been so much to take in all at once.

Over the span of a mere two days Ginny's normal, routine life had been brought to a screeching halt, and she had been packed off to her father in England. For at least half that time her mother had been on the phone.

Ginny had felt the storm brewing even before it struck. She could tell by the flat expression on her mother's face, by the tone of her voice—strained, half-whispering—as she talked on the telephone. "Can I call you back on this?" she had said. "I really have to make some arrangements." When Ginny asked what was going on, Rena had said, "I'll tell you about it later," and started dialing again.

Ginny woke up in the middle of the night to the sound of her mother's voice, still talking on the telephone. Checking her bedside clock, Ginny saw it was three-fifteen. She padded down the hall, stood outside her mother's door, and listened. "Yes, that's right," her mother was saying, her voice sounding almost frantic. "Rena Dorris. Calling from the U.S. Yes, I absolutely *do* have to talk to him today." There was a pause, then, "I understand, and I very much appreciate your going to the trouble, but it really can't wait." Ginny went into her mother's room and sat on the bed, pulling the quilt up over her legs.

When Rena finally hung up, she scooted over beside Ginny and took her daughter's hands, stroking and massaging them as she focused her thoughts. "I'm not ignoring you," she said finally, "though I know you think I am. I just wanted to get things worked out before explaining it all."

"I want to hear it now," Ginny said.

Maurice Everett's office was on the ground floor of an old building. The windows were open, and the soft drone of a distant lawn mower floated in on the air. Papers on the low bookcase under the window rustled in the breeze.

Dr. Everett was a large, sleek man, his rosy cheeks shiny, his salt-and-pepper beard as fine as silk. Ginny wondered if he blow-dried it.

"Ah, Virginia!" He greeted her heartily, leaning back in his chair and smiling. "Thank you, Roger."

"No problem," Roger said. Then: "I have the clothes in my office. Do you want them now?"

"Yes, please," Dr. Everett said. Roger ducked out.

"There's a ladies' just down the hall, so you can change in there," he told Ginny. "Then we'll be on our way. You can leave your things here."

"Can't I just wear what I have on?" Ginny asked.

Dr. Everett's laugh told her she had asked a stupid question. "No," he said. "I assure you—Iron Age people did not wear clothes like that."

Roger returned with a pile of homespun garments draped over his arm. He showed them to her piece by piece. There was a meal-colored dress with wide sleeves and a jumper to go over it. There was also a long, hooded cape for winter. The shoes, rather stiff and crude-looking, would surely give her blisters. She wondered whether they would even keep her feet dry.

Finally, and with some embarrassment, Roger handed her the underwear. It looked like a pair of men's boxer shorts, only without the elastic—it tied at the waist—and was made of coarse linen.

"Is everybody wearing this stuff?" Ginny asked.

"Indeed they are," said Dr. Everett, far too cheerfully.

Rena hadn't prepared her for this. Camping, more or less, was what she had implied. Ginny stood there, fingering the rough wool, feeling foolish.

"Go ahead, Virginia," Dr. Everett urged. "Take a left, and it's halfway down the hall."

Ginny laid the cloak on a filing cabinet before heading for the ladies' room. "I won't need this," she said. She'd be gone long before it got cold.

Dr. Everett drove a little sports car. The seats were low, so that Ginny's feet stuck straight out in front of her and she couldn't see much out the window. It was claustrophobic in there, too. Ginny realized that such cars were considered a luxury, but she couldn't imagine why. She longed to be in her mother's roomy van, perched up high and enjoying the view.

Ginny closed her eyes and silently called to her mother, half believing her thought waves could cross the Atlantic, speed over the Appalachians, fly past the bayous of Louisiana and into Rena's consciousness right there in Houston. "I want to be there with you," she telegraphed. "Let me come home."

"Mind if I smoke?" asked Maurice.

"Sort of," Ginny said without thinking.

Dr. Everett shot her a quick look of surprise, but he didn't light up. After a minute or two of uncomfortable silence he turned to her again. "How much did your father tell you about our project?"

"Nothing," she said. "I heard about it from my mom."

"Oh. Well, I think you'll find it an interesting experience."

Ginny couldn't think of anything to say to that.

"What we've done, you see, is to re-create an Iron Age farm with all the authentic buildings and tools and animals and so on—or as close as we could get to it, anyway. Now we want to see what happens when you put people into the equation."

"Like Williamsburg?" Ginny asked, picturing herself churning butter before a crowd of gawking tourists.

"Good heavens, no!" Maurice said, giving that derisive laugh again. "The farm is quite remote and protected. No, what we're doing is called experimental archaeology. Do you know what that is?"

He knew she didn't. She shook her head no.

"Well, let me give you an example. Let's say you dig up

a certain tool at an Iron Age site and to your modern eyes it looks a bit like a sickle. Curved, slender blade and all that. Okay?" he said.

"Okay," Ginny answered mechanically.

"So you put it in a museum and put a label on it saying it was used for cutting stalks of grain. That's all very well and good, but the truth is, you're just guessing. Now, imagine you have an exact replica made of that tool and take it out into the fields and try to cut grain with it. That's experimental archaeology. You may learn that it is far too light for harvesting grain but just perfect for splitting hazel wands."

"Hazel wands?" That sounded like something a fairy godmother might use.

"Slender branches of a hazel tree, Virginia. They're very supple—bend easily without snapping. The point I was trying to make is that all over Europe, back to the Middle Ages and before, people used hazel wands to make wattle constructions. And so finding such a tool would suggest that people in the Iron Age used it too. See?"

Ginny was almost afraid to ask, but she did. "What's a wattle exactly?"

Maurice sighed. He was so predictable, Ginny thought.

"Interwoven twigs or branches. You know—the way a basket is made."

"Oh," Ginny said. Clear as mud.

"It was used for just about everything from fences and baskets to the walls of buildings. The buildings, of course, were filled in with daub to make them stronger. Like mud or plaster."

Maurice looked at her pointedly, as if to make sure she was through interrupting, then plowed on. "So, anyway, our project is just that kind of thing on a grand scale. Even building the site itself was a learning process, because we know so little. You realize, of course, that there are no Iron Age buildings still standing."

Ginny nodded again. She hadn't actually thought about it ever in her life, but it seemed reasonable.

"But even a wooden structure that has rotted away long ago leaves a trace—little depressions left where the posts were set deep into the ground. The postholes give us a sort of floor plan, you see. And in addition to that, we have the accounts of Greek traders and Roman soldiers who came to Britain during the Iron Age. Among other things, both tell us that at least some of the buildings were round."

Ginny shifted around, trying to get into a more comfortable position. All she accomplished was to tighten the seat belt, the top part of which was now pressing into her neck. She hooked it awkwardly under her arm.

"We're not far now," he said. "Just about five miles to the turnoff."

"Good," Ginny said.

"Now, what was I saying?" Dr. Everett asked.

"Round buildings," Ginny prompted.

"Oh, right." He went on. "Well, you'll be living in one— a roundhouse, that is, based on Iron Age floor plans. Of course, we had to guess how tall the posts would be and then calculate the angle of the roof. As it turned out, for a cone-shaped roof to be stable and keep out the rain, it has to be at an angle of just about fifty degrees. There aren't as many options as you might think; once you start with the floor plan, everything just pretty much has to be a certain way. It's quite amazing what we've learned already."

"What are we going to do there exactly?" Ginny asked.

"Just what you would expect on a farm: tend the crops, take care of the animals, cook meals. Naturally, since you're supposed to be Iron Age peasants, you'll have to make everything you use, so we had everyone learn at least one of the crafts—spinning, weaving, tanning, making pots, that sort of thing. Except for you, of course."

Ginny noticed Maurice fumbling instinctively in his pocket for his cigarettes. Then he remembered her objection and withdrew his hand.

"It's okay," Ginny said glumly. "You can smoke."

Ginny wondered how much her mother actually knew about this Iron Age farm she was sending her to. Rena had been so anxious to get Ginny squared away she might have sent her to the space station if that's where her father had been. It was unlike Rena to be so hasty.

It reminded Ginny of a program at her school called DEAR, Drop Everything and Read. An announcement would come over the loudspeaker, and all the students would just stop what they were doing and pick up a book. Ginny didn't like it much. She already read enough on her own, and she liked her activities to progress in an orderly fashion, not jump abruptly from one thing to another. Now it occurred to Ginny that her mom had just invented her own version of that: DEAL, Drop Everything and Leave.

Ginny had a busy summer full of activities. She had a schedule. Events. Appointments. You didn't just quit all that and catch a plane.

"What about HITS?" Ginny had wailed.

"You can do HITS in the fall," Rena said, her voice tired. "I'll call Carolyn in the morning and explain."

"But they won't be doing *Fiddler on the Roof* in the fall! What about my part?"

Rena took Ginny's hands again and looked her solemnly in the eyes. "Darling, someone else will have to be Zeitel this time. Believe me, there will always be more plays—a whole lifetime of plays. But just now you need to go be with your father."

Ginny began mentally scanning the life she was being asked to abandon. "What about tennis camp?" she said. "And what about Sophie's puppies?"

"You will have to skip tennis camp," Rena said, in a voice that meant business, "and I will send you pictures of the puppies when they arrive."

Looking back now, Ginny was ashamed. That night she had wept about tennis camp and not being Zeitel and missing the birth of the puppies. She had not wept about her mother having cancer. It just hadn't seemed real somehow.

"Why?" she kept asking over and over. "Why can't I just stay here? I don't have to be looked after all the time."

Ginny had been baby-sitting for two years. If she was old enough to take care of small children, it stood to reason she was old enough to stay home alone, even if her mom was in the hospital for a few days. In fact, she could be really help-ful. She pictured herself running the house while her mother rested. Ginny would bring her Cokes and make omelets. She could go to the store on her bike. She'd have to get one of those strap-on baskets to carry the groceries in.

But her mother had just shaken her head. "No, darling, this is not the time. I need all the energy I have just to take care of myself right now. Can't you understand that? What I need for you to do is go be with your father for a while. And Ginny, dear, a trip to England—how bad can that be?"

"I just don't want to go there, okay?" she said, sounding whiny even to herself. "Couldn't I just stay with the Scotts?"

"Ginny!" her mom said, her hands on Ginny's shoulders, leaning forward to make her point. "Listen to me. I've been thinking about this for two solid days, ever since I got the first clue I had a problem. It's made me realize what a big mistake it was to let you grow up without knowing your father—"

"I know my father just fine!"

"No, precious, you really don't. And he doesn't know you either, which is a rotten shame."

"So, fine! Why do we have to worry about that now, in such a big hurry?"

Rena just looked at Ginny then, her lips slightly parted, as if she were about to speak but had suddenly frozen in the attempt. "I don't know how to say it," she said finally.

"Say what?"

"Everything comes together and points that way—"

"Points what way?" Ginny made a face of impatience.

"Toward this decision. It's summer, and you have the time, even though it means giving up things you want to do. Okay? That's the first thing. And I have to go into the hospital and will almost certainly have to have other treatment besides the surgery that will make me sick and in no shape to take care of you."

"I don't need to be taken care of!" Ginny shouted. "I'm not a baby!"

"Quit it, Ginny! I know you're not a baby. I know that if we didn't have any other choice, we could muddle through, and you'd probably be just fine, but it wouldn't be the best thing for you, and it might not even be the best thing for me."

She looked Ginny square on to make sure she had registered all this.

"Then there's the third thing. What I said before about knowing your father. The reason we need to worry about this right now, in such a hurry, is that we're not exactly knee-deep in relatives here, and if something were to happen to me, it would be real hard to be starting from scratch with your dad."

"What do you mean? What's going to happen to you?"

"Oh, Ginny! Nothing! See, that's why I didn't want to spell this out. I don't want you to jump to all kinds of wild conclusions. Just think of it as a wake-up call."

Sometimes Rena was positively incomprehensible, and Ginny suspected she probably did it on purpose—a sort of diversionary tactic.

"I want you to just trust me that your life will be considerably more enriched by spending a few weeks with Hugh Dorris than by staying here and going to tennis camp."

"And being Zeitel," Ginny reminded her.

"That too."

Rena scooped her up in a big bear hug then. They stayed that way for a very long time, Rena's cotton nightgown soft on Ginny's face, Rena's small hand stroking her back as though Ginny were still very little and had been frightened by something. Then they curled up together, under the quilt, each of them lost in her own private sorrow. After a while they slept.

"You may find things a bit hectic when you arrive," Maurice said, leaning delicately away from Ginny to blow smoke out the window. "Everyone is in the last throes of haymaking just at the minute, and it has proved to be rather more work than they had expected."

"Haymaking?" Ginny asked.

"Cutting down the tall grass, drying it, storing it away as animal fodder for the winter." He looked to see whether she comprehended this. "You're a city girl, aren't you?"

Ginny figured this was probably just a neutral observation, but somehow it felt like a put-down. It would have sounded just as scornful had he said, "You must be from the country."

"Why didn't my father come and get me?" Ginny asked, wishing she were absolutely anywhere besides in this uncomfortable car with this stuffy, silky, smoky man.

"Your father is running the project, Virginia," said Maurice. "He would have missed two whole days right in the middle of haymaking. And since they don't have a car out there, someone would have needed to drive down, pick him up, bring him back to London, drive out to the airport next day, then drive back to the farm and back to London. It really would have been a pointless lot of trouble for us as well as for Hugh."

Dr. Everett flipped his cigarette butt out the window. Ginny pictured the cigarette landing on a pile of dead grass or leaves. She turned back to look, half expecting to see smoke.

"Here's the turnoff," he said, and got out of the car to unlock a gate. He drove through, then got out again to lock it. "We're almost there," he told her.

Another five minutes down the road Maurice stopped the car and turned off the ignition. "It is possible to drive right up to the site," he told Ginny as they got out of the car, "and in fact we did so when we were delivering timbers and clay and all the animals. But now that they've gone Iron Age, it would sort of spoil the mood, so we'll walk. It's just over that rise."

The first thing Ginny thought when she saw the village was *What a dump!* The only impressive feature was the round-house, which was indeed very large. From where she stood she could scarcely see the walls, for the enormous thatched roof not only was tall but hung over the sides almost to the ground. It looked like a big, squashed, hairy tepee.

A handful of smaller buildings were scattered about the muddy compound in no apparent order, and the whole business was encompassed by a rustic fence. Dirty snow clung to the bank on which it stood and had collected in the ditch that ringed the bank.

That can't be right, Ginny realized. It's summer.

"Is that snow?" she asked doubtfully.

Maurice went, "Haw!" One thing was for sure, Ginny thought sourly: She was always good for a laugh.

"Snow!" he hooted, clearly disgusted. "That's chalk, young lady. Ancient seabeds. All this part of England is chalk with just a thin layer of topsoil over it. It's what makes the white cliffs of Dover white."

Ginny didn't know squat about the white cliffs of Dover. "Well, in Texas, dirt is brown," she shot back, and walked angrily up the path toward the compound.

Chapter 2

*H*UGH DORRIS WASN'T at the farm either. He was still in the meadow with the morning crew, cutting hay. He would be back around lunchtime.

A scruffy, hyperactive dog greeted them with high-pitched yelps and the apparent intention of knocking them down. "Shoo, Flora," Maurice scolded, pushing the dog away. A freckled young woman with auburn hair came out of the roundhouse, wiping her hands with a cloth. She bent over to pat the dog and smiled up at them.

"Ah, Karen," Maurice said, "this is Virginia." Then to Ginny: "Meet Karen Potter, our medical practitioner."

The first things Ginny noticed about Karen were that she smelled of sweat and woodsmoke and that her hair was greasy. It made Ginny wonder about the accommodations at this place. Karen didn't strike her as the kind of person who would be dirty by choice.

Karen led Ginny into the roundhouse. It was cool and

dark inside, the air hazy from the central cook fire, the odor of smoke very pronounced. Looking up, Ginny could see the architecture of the roof, the long rafters rising to join at the central peak, a crude ring beam stabilizing the structure about halfway up. She found it hard to imagine anyone building such a colossal thing by hand.

"This is my husband, Mark," Karen said, indicating a slim, bearded man sitting on the far side of the fire, turning the handles of a grinding stone. He looked to Ginny like a street person, his hair wild and unkempt, his beard untrimmed, his skin dry and baked by the sun.

"Welcome to the Iron Age, Virginia," Mark said. He had a very nice voice. His accent wasn't crisp and stuffy like Dr. Everett's. You could tell he had a sense of humor.

"Ginny," she said.

"Ginny it is," said Mark.

She walked over to where he was sitting. Flora had followed them inside and now curled up near Mark as if returning to an interrupted nap.

"What are you doing?" Ginny asked.

"Well," he said, "I'm grinding wheat on a rotary quern. To make bread."

"I can do that," said Ginny. "My mom and I make bread every week."

"Well, that's good," Karen said brightly, "because your dad could certainly do with some help in that department."

"My dad bakes bread?" Ginny asked, incredulous.

"We have a cooking rota," Karen said. "Everybody

cooks. Everybody bakes bread. Today it's Mark and me, tomorrow Faith and Bennett, and so on. It's very democratic."

"Actually, now that Ginny's here, I think we ought to change the rota," Mark said. "Ginny with her dad. Enough with the bachelor brigade."

"What's that?" asked Ginny.

Karen laughed. "Oh, you know, since your dad is single and all, and the job is really too much for one person, we matched him up with the only other spare adult—"

"In a manner of speaking," Mark added.

"Well, okay, he's almost an adult," Karen said. "Corey Donnelley—he's seventeen. Anyway, at the risk of sounding sexist, they are both absolutely hopeless in the cooking department. Particularly with the bread, I'm afraid. You will be a welcome addition, I assure you."

"Maybe you shouldn't change things too much," Ginny said. "I won't be here long."

All this time Maurice had been pacing about the roundhouse restlessly, fingering the various objects—baskets, pots, sheepskins—that lay about, as if he were browsing in an antiques shop. Finally he glanced pointedly at his watch and muttered, "I must be getting back. Why don't you show Ginny her room and so forth?"

"Will do," said Mark. "See you in about a week?"

"Six days," Maurice said. "I'm off then. Cheerio."

Ginny waved silently, a fake smile plastered on her face, then suddenly ran after him. "Dr. Everett," she called. "My bag!"

He stopped, looking perplexed. "Your suitcase, you mean?" He raised his eyebrows.

"Yes. Is it still in the car?"

After a slight pause he said, "No, it's back at the university. In storage."

"In storage! I've got all my stuff in there. My toothbrush and shampoo and all that."

Maurice spread his hands wide and gazed upward as if asking God why He had landed him with this impenetrable idiot. "Nobody . . . has . . . stuff . . . here," he said slowly. "No stuff at all."

"I can't even brush my teeth?" she wailed. "I can't wash my hair?"

"Karen will fill you in," he said, and strode off in the direction of the car.

"You'll get used to it," Karen assured her. "I suppose we'll all smell a bit ripe to you at first, though." She laughed easily.

"It's okay," Ginny said glumly.

"We do brush our teeth actually," Karen added, taking Ginny's hand. "With a hazel twig. Chew on the end a bit, and it gets bristly. Makes a very respectable toothbrush."

"Okay," she said again. She didn't want to talk about it anymore. "Can I see my room?" she asked.

"Of course," Karen said, "though 'room' may be gilding the lily a bit."

All around the perimeter of the roundhouse Ginny saw a system of wicker partitions made of interwoven hazel wands. Cloaks and sheepskins had been draped over them, perhaps to provide a bit of privacy. The partitions were so loosely woven you could see right through them. Later Ginny realized there was another reason. They hung things there because there wasn't anywhere else to put them.

The cubicle she would share with her father was the size of her mother's bedroom closet. Like the rest of the round-house, it had a dirt floor and was very dark. It smelled of smoke and dust. To her right as she stepped inside were two primitive bunk beds, the heads attached to the outside wall, the feet toward the hearth. The far side of the beds abutted the dividing partition.

"I seriously doubt they had bunk beds in the Iron Age," Karen said, "but we had already set up the rooms, and Hugh's was designed for only one person. There wasn't space to add a second bed at ground level."

Ginny went over to the bottom bed and felt around. There was a mattress of braided straw and on top of that a simple sleeping bag made of sheepskins sewn together, wool-ly side in. An extra sheepskin was rolled up to make a pillow.

Normally she would have asked for the top bunk. It was the cool place to be. But this was an entirely different mat-ter. Here the upper bunk was fixed to the wall just a foot below the point where the roof beams met the upright poles. It would be like sleeping in a cave, she thought. And the thatch, so close to her face, was sure to be crawling with bugs.

Suddenly Ginny felt cornered. She didn't want to be in this weird place with these strange people while back in Houston her real life went on without her and Rena lay sick in a hospital. But what could she do? Walk to London? Call her mom collect and ask her to arrange a ticket? Hitch a ride to the airport dressed as an Iron Age peasant? It struck her more than ever before how grown-ups had all the power. They had money and credit cards and cars. Kids were stuck wherever you put them. Ginny began to cry.

"I want to go home," she sobbed. "I just want to go home."

About an hour later the haymaking crew began straggling into the clearing. They balanced enormous baskets of hay on their backs, which forced them into awkward, hunched-over postures. They approached in a steady, plodding manner, exhaustion apparent with every step.

Ginny and Karen stood outside waiting, their poses identical, left hands arched over left eyes to shield them from the sun. Now that Ginny was about to see her father, she began to grow nervous. It had been well over a year since she'd seen him last, and that had been for only a few days. He had come to Boston for a professional conference, after which he had flown out to Houston and rented a hotel suite so they could stay together. The idea was to give them more time for a really good visit. But mostly they just hung out and watched television or went down to the pool. He would sit in a lounge chair and read while Ginny went into the water. Swimming alone wasn't all that much fun, she discovered. She tried showing him some of her dives, but every time she got up on the board he was looking down at his book.

The next day Ginny asked if her friend Andrea could come over. Hugh said that was fine. Ginny suspected he was relieved; they were having a hard time making conversation. Andrea stayed all day, and they played Marco Polo and Drop the Monkey in the pool till they got waterlogged, then went to the exercise room and played on the equipment. By the time the attendant shooed them out, Hugh had gone back up to the room.

They had planned to eat at the pricey rooftop restaurant that night, but Andrea hadn't brought the right clothes. So instead they had gone out for Mexican food.

Ginny felt ill at ease with her dad, but she was rather proud of him too. He seemed such an exotic creature with his movie star British accent and Indiana Jones profession. She wanted Andrea to be impressed. So she was horribly disappointed when Hugh ordered the most unimaginative thing on the menu, the combination plate—one taco, two enchiladas, rice, beans, and guacamole.

"Well, I want the cabrito," Ginny said in an effort to restore the family's reputation for worldly sophistication. "Goat meat," she told Andrea knowingly.

The next morning, when Hugh dropped Ginny off on his way to the airport, he hugged her hard. His voice almost seemed to break as he said good-bye. It puzzled Ginny that he should seem so moved to part from her when he so rarely wrote or visited and had so little to say when he did.

The first couple to trudge into the compound was accompanied by a small child. Their approach had been fascinating to watch, because the little girl kept dancing around their feet, wailing and shrieking in a high-pitched voice. Once or twice she threw her arms around her mother's legs, though Ginny couldn't be sure whether the girl meant to embrace her mother or trip her up.

"Oh, dear," Karen said, "Daisy's in a state."

"The little girl?" Ginny asked.

"Yeah. She's fine most of the time around the compound if you give her something to do. But this haymaking business is too much for her."

"They're making her work in the fields?" Ginny asked, astounded.

"No, of course not. But she has to go out there where her parents can watch her. When she's hot enough and bored enough, she gets like that."

The couple was busy setting down their loads. "Mind your feet," the woman warned the little girl as she shifted her huge basket around. Daisy stepped away dramatically, folding her arms and sticking out her lower lip. Then she stomped her foot for emphasis, as if she just wanted to make sure nobody missed that she was mad.

"Cute," Ginny said.

"Yeah," agreed Karen, "it's a problem. Come on and meet Liz and Tom."

Now that they were standing upright, Ginny could see what they looked like. Despite windblown hair, silly clothes, and sweaty, sunburned faces, the Fieldings were the handsomest people she had ever seen in real life. Tom was a huge man, perhaps six-five, with broad shoulders and a noble brow. Smiling tiredly, he brushed his forelock back with a massive hand. The gesture made Ginny weak with admiration.

Liz looked at least six feet tall, slim and muscular with olive skin and honey-streaked hair. It blew picturesquely in the wind. Ginny felt like she had wandered into a really strange fashion shoot.

"This is Hugh's daughter, Ginny," Karen said, and they shook hands all around. Tom's grip was gentle, his big hand dry and leathery. Ginny felt an unaccountable impulse to stroke it.

Daisy had been momentarily distracted into silence by Ginny's appearance, but now she shifted back into full gear. Taking firm hold of Tom's baggy trousers, she tried to shake him, really throwing her weight into it. This had no effect besides messing up his clothes. He pretended to look annoyed, then reached down and scooped her up, lifting her high in the air with his powerful arms. Daisy squealed with delight. "And this," he said proudly, "is Daisy!"

The Munsons, Ian and Millie, dragged in next. They were as small and dark as the Fieldings were tall and fair, but they were every bit as fit. That was not surprising, Ginny decided. Nobody would sign up for a project like this who wasn't in pretty good shape.

"Hugh will be along soon," Millie said, sighing heavily and pressing hand to chest in a gesture of weariness. "I know he's dying to see you."

People always said what they thought you wanted to

hear, Ginny mused, and they meant to make you feel good. But a lot of times it had the opposite effect. If he was so anxious to see her, why had she been picked up at the airport by some frog-eyed graduate student? Driven here by that officious professor with the cigarettes? Why did her father have to be the very last person to come in from the meadow?

With still no sight of Hugh, a fourth family arrived. They were part of the afternoon crew and had spent the morning gathering wild plants, a restful occupation, to save their strength for the grueling work to come. The Kirklands had two boys, about eight and ten, Ginny guessed. The boys, Sam and Nat, had no shirts on and were covered from bare feet to shaggy heads with a substantial coating of fine dust, which ran in places where they had sweated. They looked like creatures raised by wolves.

The parents of the wild children were introduced as Bunny and Jonas. They seemed a bit older than the rest, perhaps in their early forties. Both of them had a fair amount of gray in their hair.

Jonas shook Ginny's hand distractedly, turning to shout at his children in a booming voice. He had rather wild eyebrows, thick and curly, giving him an eccentric look. "Nice to have you here," he said, thumping her heartily on the shoulder, then heading off to other things.

"You do look just like your dad," said Bunny, who assumed this was a welcome comment. "What a treat to see a new face too." She smiled in an odd way that pushed up her cheeks and caused her eyes to squeeze into little slits.

Ginny wondered whether this rabbity smile had landed her with Bunny as a nickname, or if that was the actual name on her birth certificate.

The compound had seemed quiet and empty when Ginny arrived. Now it buzzed with life. People spread out in different directions, getting drinks of water, washing hands, disappearing into the roundhouse, and—in the case of Nat and Sam—running over to snort at the pigs. Ginny just stood there, the unmoving center of all this activity, waiting.

"There he is!" Karen shouted, pointing in the direction of the path to the meadow, where a tall figure plodded along steadily, bent under his load of hay. Ginny suddenly realized that for the past half hour Karen had been hovering nearby—out of politeness, or was it pity?—so Ginny wouldn't have to wait alone.

As Hugh came nearer, Ginny saw that indeed, she might not have recognized him if he had been at the airport. His ash brown hair was long and uncombed, and he had grown a beard. He looked gaunt, as though he'd lost about ten pounds.

Hugh spotted Ginny and waved airily as he came through the gate. All smiles, he made a brief gesture to indicate his load, went about lowering it to the ground, then held out his arms.

As she stepped into his embrace, Ginny suddenly realized how much she had counted on this moment. She had actually believed that her father could shift her world back into place, so that she would no longer feel lost and alone but protected and cherished. It had been a lot to hope for. What she felt now was only distaste at touching his sweaty skin, smelling his body odor, feeling his scratchy beard against her cheek. She didn't feel better now that he was here; she felt a whole lot worse.

Chapter 3

*L*UNCH WAS WELL under way when the last of the villagers arrived. Since the weather was fine, everyone was eating outside on the semicircle of logs near the entrance to the roundhouse. From a distance they could see the little group strolling up the path toward the compound. There were three of them, a young couple and a teenage boy. Ginny thought the boy must be Corey, her father's cooking partner.

Karen said they had gone down to the river to try their hands at fishing. Apparently they had been unsuccessful.

"Behold! The fisherpersons return!" Mark called out.

"But where are all the fish?" several hecklers added as the three came through the gate.

"We hooked a big one," said the man, "but when we pulled it out of the water, it spoke to us, so we had to let it go."

"Oh, really?" said Liz, a suppressed smile tugging at the corners of her mouth. "What did it say?"

"It said we could have three wishes. As a reward, you know, for setting it free."

Daisy was enthralled by this story, believing it to be the real honest truth. She left her seat on the log and ran to the man who was speaking.

"What did you wish?" she asked breathlessly.

"Well . . . ," he said with tantalizing slowness, then turned to his wife. "What was that first wish?"

The wife pressed her thin lips together in a thoughtful manner. The story was only for Daisy now. "I think you wished that lunch would be ready when we got back."

Daisy screamed in horror. Such a wasted wish!

"And then what was that second one?"

Daisy bounced up and down in a display of fierce excitement.

"The second wish was . . . that Hugh's daughter would be here."

Daisy turned briefly in Ginny's direction, her face showing vividly how unworthy she was of that second wish.

Daisy had begun to feed on too much excitement and too much attention. She was losing control. Liz got up and took her hand. "It's just a story," she whispered.

Daisy wrenched her hand away. "What was the last wish?" she demanded.

"Let me think," said the woman. "Corey, do you remember?"

Corey glanced away, embarrassed. He was really good-looking, Ginny thought, with black hair and a very pale, fine complexion. She noticed a dimple on the side of his nose and two more on his earlobe, the remains of piercing recently abandoned. Ginny pictured him wearing a nose ring and two earrings. He would need a black leather jacket to go with it.

"I remember now," the woman went on. "I wished Daisy would give me a kiss!" She leaned over and offered her cheek.

Daisy slapped her hips with both hands, stomped her feet. Liz dragged her back to her place on the log. "She's only five, Faith," she said to the woman. "You really shouldn't wind her up like that."

"You thought it was funny when she started," Corey snapped back.

Everybody stared. There was an edge to his voice and a challenge in his look.

"Let it be, Corey," Hugh said. Then, before Corey could answer back, Hugh plunged into introductions. "Ginny," he said, "I want you to meet Bennett and Faith Clark and Faith's brother, Corey Donnelley. My daughter, Ginny Dorris."

Faith and Bennett came over and shook hands. Corey just nodded his head with half-closed eyes. It was a very sexy look, Ginny thought.

"We considered eating your lunch since you were late but decided against it," said Karen, a little too cheery, anxious to smooth things over. She got up and led them into the roundhouse.

Ginny resumed nibbling on her bread, a dense, flat loaf. It wasn't much like regular bread—it was more like a big, chewy biscuit and tasted faintly of woodsmoke—but then Mark and Karen hadn't had all that much to work with. Just coarse stone-ground flour, water, and salt. It was unleavened because Iron Age people had had no yeast. Nor were there eggs to put in the dough. Though the village had almost forty hens, they were of an old English variety, and none of them had laid much after the first clutch in the spring.

Tearing off a bit of the bread, Ginny scooped up a dollop of soft white cheese from the small wooden bowl in her lap. It was freshly made goat cheese, flavored with wild garlic, and though different from the kind her mother bought at home, it was tangy and good. Karen had given her a taste earlier. When Ginny said she liked it, Karen had said that it was a good thing. She'd be having a lot of it.

Ginny used her finger to scoop up the last bits of cheese that clung to the edge of the bowl. Sensing something, she looked up. Corey was still standing there, watching her. Ginny gave him a *what's-it-to-ya?* stare. Then she licked her finger and wiped the spit off on her skirt.

Corey laughed at that and went inside the roundhouse.

Ginny spent the afternoon wandering restlessly about the compound while others worked. Mark and Karen were busy making stew, fetching water and wood, and grinding more wheat for the breakfast porridge. That would be the last task of the night, Karen told her: to set the mixture of cracked grain and water over the coals to cook slowly overnight.

Others were busy loading hay onto one of the six

hayricks, tall, upright poles set in the ground with low wooden platforms circling them. The platforms were there to protect the bottom sheaves from the wet ground so they wouldn't rot. The poles kept the piles straight and also supported the little thatched roofs that kept the hay dry.

Ginny felt at loose ends, so she went to look for her dad. She found him in the roundhouse, constructing a forge. The spot he had chosen was near the front door, presumably so some of the smoke would float outside, rather than adding to the considerable smog already produced by the hearth and the bread oven. So far his forge consisted of a large pit lined with clay, where the fire would go. He was now in the process of constructing a wind tunnel, through which air from the bellows would be channeled right into the heart of the fire, increasing the temperature.

Hugh had already made the bellows. He showed them to Ginny with obvious pride, explaining how much work they represented. "Every job, no matter how simple it seems, was an endless series of steps for Iron Age people," he said. "They couldn't just make a thing—first they had to make the tools to make it with."

The bellows were a perfect example. More than a month before, a goat had been slaughtered. Millie Munson, the village tanner, had scraped the hide free of hair, fat, and membrane, then soaked it in a solution of alum and salt for a few weeks. It then had to be stretched on a frame to dry, cleaned, and scraped again, until finally it was ready to use. All this had to be done before Hugh could have the two triangular pieces of leather for the sides of his bellows.

Meanwhile, he had spent many hours carving two flat shapes out of wood for the top and bottom as well as a slender tube for the small end. With an iron punch he made small holes along the edges of the wood for attaching the leather sections.

The final step had been to sew it all together. Of course, before he could do that, he had to carve a needle out of bone, a task that took him a good half day, and spin wool into thread. And to get the wool, someone had to shear the sheep.

"Amazing, isn't it?" Hugh said. He used his hands expressively as he talked, clearly excited by his bellows and the history of their creation.

Ginny couldn't help thinking that after all that work the bellows didn't look that great. They reminded her of the potholders and ashtrays she had produced in kindergarten: crude and ugly but made with loving hands.

"What about all that stuff?" she asked, indicating the tongs and hammers and hatchets and knives hanging from hooks on the wall. "Did you make those?"

"No," he said. "Maurice had a blacksmith make them; they're copies of museum models from Iron Age sites. I'm going to make some tools of my own once the forge is set up, though," he added.

He had turned positively radiant, like a different person. She realized, of course, that what he was really excited about was Iron Age blacksmithing, but it felt like he was interested in her.

"Well . . . ," he said, suddenly run out of steam, and picked up a branch of hazel, bending it carefully to test its suppleness. He returned his attention to building the support for the clay tunnel.

"Dad," Ginny asked, "is there a telephone around here?"

"What?" He was not following her train of thought.

"A phone. To call Mom. So I can find out how she is. So I'll know when it's time to go home."

"Oh," said Hugh. "Well, Maurice will come out and tell us if there are any messages. That's how she contacted me in the first place. She telephoned Maurice, and he came out and told me."

Ginny thought that sounded like an arrangement set up for emergencies. What she wanted to do was make a regular call, to hear the sound of her mother's voice and find out how the surgery had gone, what the doctors had said. It especially bothered her that the person who would carry her mother's messages was a man she disliked and who thought she was a fool.

"I need to talk to Mom," she said again.

Hugh didn't answer right away. Ginny could see he was somewhere else, considering the stability and form of his wind tunnel. He fastened the arched hazel wand carefully with a slender strip of leather, then looked up. His face was blank. What had she asked? Oh, yes.

"Ginny, your mother is probably in surgery as we speak—or just recovering. I doubt she could take a call."

"Well, I don't mean right this minute. But tomorrow, maybe, or the next day."

"I think you should just let her be right now. Your mother has her hands full."

"I hate that!" Ginny said.

"What?" said Hugh, astonished.

She mimicked him in a singsong voice, "Your mother has her hands full!" and made a face. "Like if I called her, it would be some kind of burden. Isn't that what people are supposed to do when somebody's sick? Call and send flowers and show they care? You think it would bother her for me to call?"

Hugh made a little sound of disgust. "Oh, cut it out," he said.

"Answer my question," Ginny insisted defiantly.

He gave her a hard look. "Ginny, you're her child. It's her job to take care of you. So if you start phoning her a lot, she'll start worrying about you and thinking about your problems when she has more than she can do to deal with her own. She's turned all that over to me for the moment."

Ginny felt like something was stuck in her throat. "She misses me when I'm not there. Talking to me would make her happy. She loves me."

There wasn't much she could do after that but walk away, so she did.

"I'm sorry about your mother," Karen said. She was kneeling, bent over, pouring water onto her hair. She had stripped to the waist, and her small breasts bobbled around as she worked. Ginny had never seen a grown woman take off her clothes in public before. When she asked about it, Karen shrugged. She said she didn't want to get her dress wet.

"How do you know about my mother?" Ginny asked.

"Hugh told us, to explain why you were coming."

"She has breast cancer," Ginny said.

"Yes, I know."

It struck Ginny that this was the first time she had actually said those words out loud. She wondered whether that was bad luck. No, she thought, it was bad luck to expect the best. That's what people called "tempting fate."

"How old is your mom?" Karen asked.

It seemed like a strange question. Ginny had to think a minute. "Thirty . . . six? Thirty-seven? Gosh, I don't know exactly."

"Young," said Karen.

Rena didn't seem all that young to Ginny, just a regular age for a mom.

"Any family history?"

"Family history?"

"Of breast cancer. Like your mother's sister or maybe her mother."

"She doesn't have a sister, and I don't know about my grandmother. She died way back before I was born. Why?"

"Oh, I just wondered. It's one of the risk factors."

"Is that why you asked how old she is? Is that a risk factor too?

"Well, it's more usual in older women."

Ginny didn't quite see what point Karen was trying to make. She was about to ask when Karen reached down and took a fistful of red clay and began rubbing it into her wet hair.

"What are you doing?" Ginny cried.

Karen chuckled behind her curtain of hair. "Having a shampoo," she said.

"With dirt?"

"Not dirt; clay," corrected Karen. "Haven't you ever seen women put clay masks on their faces?"

"No," said Ginny.

"Well, they do. It's a beauty treatment. The clay absorbs oil and tightens the pores. They sell it at the chemist's."

"But on your hair?"

"Sure. It takes out the oil. It's the best thing we've come up with so far."

"Why can't you use soap?"

"We haven't done all that well with soap, I'm afraid. We followed the traditional recipes, but the result was pretty nasty. You wouldn't want to wash anything with it, trust me on that."

"Gosh," said Ginny. "I thought people in the olden days always made their own soap and candles and things. I would think it was pretty easy."

"Go ahead—rub it in," Karen said. "Actually it's been very humbling, finding out how unskilled we are. If you can believe it, we couldn't even start a fire our first day. Maurice had to get it going with a cigarette lighter!"

She began rinsing out the clay, dribbling on small amounts of water from the bucket, then rubbing to dissolve the clay. It was a messy operation. Ginny could see why she had pulled down the top of her dress.

"Would it help if I poured the water over your head for you?" Ginny asked.

"Yes, please. Not too much water at a time. Give me a chance to work it in. That's it." Ginny poured till the bucket was empty.

"Should I go get some more?" There was definitely still clay in Karen's hair.

"That would be lovely. But don't get it out of the well. It's too cold. There's a tub of water in the roundhouse. Mark's warming it for our bath. Why don't you bring me some of that?"

Ginny went in the back door so she wouldn't have to walk past her father. She found Mark standing over a half barrel full of water, stirring it with a long pair of iron tongs. A plume of steam rose from the water where the tongs went in.

"What's that?" Ginny asked.

Mark lifted the tongs out to show her a lump of metal. "Pot boiler," he said, putting it back in. "Very hot."

"Can I have some of that water?" Ginny asked. "I'm helping Karen rinse her hair."

"Be my guest." He pulled the tongs out again while she filled the pail.

"Everybody isn't going to take a bath in that same water, are they?" Ginny asked.

"Nope," said Mark, and she could see from his grin that she had said something funny. "Just Karen and me. *You* get to bathe on your cooking day."

Ginny just stood there a minute, mentally calculating the number of families. She counted six. One bath every six days. No wonder everybody smelled.

Ginny went back outside.

From a distance she saw Karen kneeling patiently in the scrubby grass, her head and shoulders bent gracefully forward, hair dripping, the afternoon sunlight playing across her bare back. Ginny thought she looked beautiful, like someone in a painting.

Ginny resumed dribbling water over Karen's head but found the task a bit harder with a full bucket. The water tended to run down the side and dribble on her shoes.

The dog, Flora, sat quietly watching them in an abstracted way, as if absorbed in working out some thorny problem.

"Maurice said you were a medical practitioner," Ginny said after a while. "Does that mean you're a doctor?"

"I'm a nurse actually," Karen said. "So I'm in charge of any medical problems that might come up. That's what he meant."

"So you know all about cancer?" Ginny asked.

"Well, some things," Karen said. "What do you want to know?" Karen wrung out her hair like a washcloth, then sat up. Seeing Ginny look away embarrassed, Karen slid her dress back on.

What did she want to know? Ginny wasn't sure. Her mother had already told her plenty on the hourlong drive to the airport. She had explained about the operation to remove her breast and check her lymph nodes. She had talked about chemotherapy and how it would make her sick and weak for a while and how she might lose her hair. Ginny didn't want to hear those things; they made her squirm to think about. She had found herself half listening, blocking out the details.

After checking Ginny in for her flight, Rena walked with her to the departure gate, explaining all the way about what would happen on the other end: passport control and going through customs. Ginny didn't need to be told these things. She and her mother had taken lots of trips. Rena was just talking to make herself feel better about sending Ginny away.

The departure lounge had been so crowded with travelers that they had trouble finding two seats together. Most of them were families going on vacation. Together. Ginny envied them increasingly as she and her mother sat side by side for the next forty minutes, completely run out of conversation. When it was announced that the flight was boarding, Ginny was relieved.

Ginny looked into Karen's searching gaze and realized that she was waiting for her question. But when Ginny tried to think of one, it suddenly struck her: She didn't want to hear one more word about cancer. Ever again, if possible.

"Karen," she said, "how can you tell what day it is?"

"Pardon?"

"I mean—you don't have a calendar or anything out here, do you? My school starts on August twenty-first," she said.

"Oh," Karen said. "That early?" She gazed thoughtfully at the ground for a while, idly tracing a figure eight in the dirt. Or maybe it was the sign for infinity. "Ginny," she said after a while, "can I give you some advice?"

"Okay," said Ginny reluctantly. When people talked like

that, something unpleasant usually followed.

"Try letting go of it."

"What?"

"The thing with your mother. You can't do anything about it, you know. It isn't in your power. And you can't see into the future either. Sometimes you just have to wait and see what happens."

"I can't stop thinking about it, though."

"I know it's hard," Karen said, getting to her feet, "but you need to think about something else." She touched Ginny's nose with her fingertip and gave her a tender smile. "Find yourself some work to do," she said, and walked away with the bucket.

After dinner Ginny wandered around the compound until she found a split log with a wide, flat side. She took a fist-size rock and rubbed the log briskly, hoping to smooth the surface. She wasn't too successful but decided eventually that it was good enough.

Inside the roundhouse she took the iron punch and laid its tip in the coals. While she waited for it to heat up, she calculated mentally. It had been a Tuesday when she left. Tuesday, July 14. So that would make this the evening of Wednesday, the fifteenth.

When the tip of the punch was hot, Ginny began burning a crude *S* on the top left-hand part of the log. She had done this at camp, burning Indian symbols into a leather belt. This tool wasn't as good, and the results were messy, but she kept at it. She began burning an *M* right next to it but had to reheat her tool halfway through. This was going to take a long time.

"What are you doing?" Her father bent over to get a good look.

"I'm making a calendar," she said.

"Interesting," he said, standing upright again. "None of us thought of that. It's really very appropriate. All the early civilizations were quite observant of the phases of the moon and the position of the stars and such, so they could make calendars. To know when to plant their crops and when to hold their festivals."

"I just want to know when I can go home," Ginny said.

Chapter 4

THE NEXT MORNING was overcast with dark, threatening clouds off to the west. Out in the meadow, grass cut the day before lay in heaps, drying. With a storm coming, the villagers needed to bring in as much of it as they could, and right away. A thorough soaking would ruin it. Armed with rakes and poles, the entire village hurried off to the task. Even Jonas and the boys came, though it was their cooking day.

Karen showed Ginny how to turn the hay, revealing its green underside to the air and releasing its sweet summer smell. Not far away, a larger group was busy loading the driest hay into baskets and carrying it back to the compound. They worked silently, focused on speed.

The wind picked up after the first hour. It felt good on Ginny's sweaty skin but added to the sense of urgency. It meant the rain would be there soon.

"Isn't this kind of a waste of time?" Ginny asked Karen. "Shouldn't we just gather it up and carry it back?"

"We couldn't carry very much in our arms," she said, "and we don't have enough baskets." She leaned on her rake and checked out what the others were doing. "The hay over on that side takes first priority. It's already dry and ready to go. Maybe you're right—we ought to go help them with the loading, instead of doing this," she said. "Come on."

They found Liz standing immobile in a sea of energetic motion, a squinty frown on her face, her lower lip pinned down by a row of straight white teeth. She seemed to be looking for something. "Have you seen Daisy?" she asked as they approached.

"No," said Karen. "Not since we got here."

"Maybe she went back to the compound," said Jonas with a grunt, bending to his work.

"Maybe," Karen said doubtfully. "Hugh," she called to Ginny's dad, who was already on his way back with a load, "could you check to see if Daisy's there?"

"Be glad to," he said, and strode up the path with his basket heaped high. Bits of hay drifted off it in the wind.

The work went on efficiently, reminding Ginny of a bucket brigade. Some fanned out and gathered the hay on the periphery, bringing it toward the center. There, near the baskets, stood the loaders, who scooped it up and packed it away. Both jobs meant constant stooping and bending. Ginny knew she would be sore in the morning.

Nat and Sam threw themselves into the job with wild excitement, gathering small handfuls of hay and raining them down on the heads of the basket loaders.

"On the ground," shouted Millie with irritation, "not on our heads!" They ran off again, giggling.

"And see if you can bring a little more next time," Karen called after them. "Be useful."

Ian returned, having delivered his load. Like vultures on a dead rabbit, the crew circled the empty basket and began filling it. The sky was really dark now—like night was coming on. It felt kind of creepy, Ginny thought.

"Did you see Daisy at the compound?" Liz asked.

"No, but I wasn't looking for her," Ian said. "She gone missing?"

"Yes," said Liz, more annoyance than fear in her voice.

"You want me to go back and look?"

"No, Hugh said he would."

Ginny tried to think where Daisy would go. She was inclined to sulk in corners when she was upset, and on a day like this one, with everybody too busy to pay her much attention, she might have gone off somewhere, hoping to be found and fussed over. The compound seemed the obvious place.

Ginny and her friend Jessica had hidden under the bed once because Rena had said Jessica couldn't spend the night. Ginny's infantile logic told her that if they couldn't be found when it was time to drive Jessica home, it would seem easier just to let her stay. They were under there for several hours and heard Rena calling frantically. Even when the police came, and the girls saw those black, shiny police shoes walking around the room, Ginny wanted to stay put. Jessica, having more sense, scooted out and gave herself up.

About a minute later her mother's face appeared as, on hands and knees, she peered into the darkness at her daughter. "You might want to stay there for a while," she said hoarsely, "because right now I'm really, really mad!"

She had stayed there too.

"No sign of her!" called Hugh as he trotted back down the path. He slung the basket down, and the vultures descended. "Shall we send out a search party?"

"Did you look in our cubicle?" asked Liz.

"Yes," he said.

The wind whipped up again, and a few drops hit their faces. "Oh, no!" said Hugh. "Hurry!"

Liz turned to Ginny. "Would you go see if you can find her?" she said, raking her fingers through her beautiful hair. "I really can't leave just now."

Ginny sighed. "How hard did you look?" she asked her dad, trying to decide whether to retrace his steps.

"Well, I checked in the roundhouse, looked in the Fieldings' cubicle, glanced around the compound. I mean, there aren't that many places she could be that I wouldn't have seen her."

"How about the lavatory?" suggested Karen.

"Yes, I looked there."

It was as she suspected—the minimum effort. It probably hadn't even occurred to him that Daisy wouldn't pop right out when she was called.

"Okay," she said, scooping up an armful of hay and heading up the path to the compound. It seemed wasteful to make the trip empty-handed.

She tried to remember being five and up to no good. Where would she have hidden? She searched all the cubicles, under the beds, behind storage baskets, even in the henhouse. Bunny, who was busy trying to get the fire going in the bread oven, said Daisy hadn't been there all morning.

A flash of lightning lit the growing darkness, followed quickly by a great boom of thunder. It made Ginny nervous. Concentrate, she told herself. If Daisy wasn't here, where else would she go? Was she hiding in the long grass somewhere? In the sheep meadow? What if she had just wandered away and was lost?

From the top of the path, where it sloped down toward the meadow, she stopped and searched the landscape. Below, little figures in beige and brown moved about like busy bugs. They were almost the same color as the dried grass. Daisy would be, too, Ginny realized. In her oatmeal-colored dress she would be hard to see. If only she were dressed in scarlet.

Ginny studied the uncut grass on the far side of the meadow. The wind swept across it in waves, like the sea. There was no break in the pattern large enough to be a child. Daisy wasn't there. She turned her attention to the sheep meadow. Daisy could blend in there too. Ginny had to look at every sheep separately to make sure, but eventually she felt certain there was nothing there but sheep and grass. She sensed instinctively that a child wouldn't wade into the tall wheat and barley and oats that grew in the near-by fields. No, there was just one place left: the woods.

The wind was coming in great gusts now, and more fat drops of rain splattered on her head and shoulders. Ginny ran toward the sheltering trees.

"Daisy!" she called at the top of her lungs. "Hurry, quick, before the storm comes!"

It was dark in there, with no sunlight to filter through the canopy. Menacing almost. Ginny half expected to see grotesque faces appear on the trunks of the gnarled trees, like in picture books, and the branches to reach out like bony fingers to snatch her away.

"Daisy! Are you in here?"

Ginny was starting to panic. How could she comb an entire forest? What if she searched for hours, then came back soaking wet only to discover that Daisy had long ago turned up? "Oh, we found her," Liz would say.

As Ginny made her way along the path, the distant rush of running water brought an alarming thought. Until now she had felt pretty sure that while Daisy might be lost, at least she was in no danger. Now Ginny remembered the river. Corey's family had gone fishing there; it would have to be substantial. Ginny began to trot. "Daisy!" she called, her voice wavering as she ran.

Overhead in the canopy she could hear the rain coming down hard. Again a boom of thunder startled her.

In a lightning storm do not stand under a tree. Did a whole forest count?

She could see the river now. It was wide enough to create a gap in the canopy, and the rain pelted the surface of the water with a million fat drops, making tiny waves and bubbles and a good deal of noise. Daisy wasn't there.

"Daisy!" Ginny screamed again, so loud that her voice broke. For just a few seconds the rain let up, and she thought she heard a whimper. Ginny called again. This time she was sure.

It was coming from farther upstream. Leaving the path, she traipsed through leaves and mud, following the riverbank. Ginny's wet hair was plastered to her face, big drops rolling down into her eyes. Her wet shoes flopped loosely as she walked, threatening to trip her with every step. She felt suddenly, horribly miserable.

Then, as she rounded a copse of trees overhanging the river, she stopped and gaped. On the far side of the copse stood a very small Iron Age roundhouse. It was made of wattle, just like everything back at the compound, only not nearly so well constructed. It had once had a roof of branches covered with dried grass, most of which had fallen in. Through the gaps in the wicker Ginny could see Daisy sitting, knees clasped to chest, head down.

Ginny knelt at the doorway and reached inside. "Come on out, Daisy. It's storming like crazy. Let's go back where it's safe and dry."

Daisy looked up. Her face was a dreadful mess of mud and snot. There was a look in her pale eyes—terror mixed with utter hopelessness—that made Ginny catch her breath.

"Come on, sweetie," she crooned. "Your mom is worried."

Daisy uncurled herself slowly.

"That's right. Come on out."

"I want Nancy," Daisy said through big sobs.

"We'll talk about it on the way," Ginny urged. "Come on."

Daisy crawled through the door on all fours, then stood. Her dress was soaked with mud. Ginny took her hand, struck by how tiny it was.

"Who built your little house?" Ginny asked, leading Daisy back toward the path.

"Nat and Sam," she said, with little hiccuping gasps of sorrow between the words. "And me too."

"Really?" Ginny said. "Is this your special place?

"Sometimes."

"Who's Nancy?" It was slow going with Daisy's small steps. Ginny had to resist the temptation to race ahead.

"My nanny," she said.

"Oh," said Ginny. "She takes care of you at home?"

"Yes," Daisy said. "She lives with us. But she's not here."

"And you miss her very much?"

"Yes," she said again.

They had reached the path at last. Ginny stopped for a moment and took off her shoes. They were worse than useless.

"Don't forget—you've got your mom and dad here," Ginny pointed out in her best Pollyanna manner.

"They go to school all the time," she said.

Tom was getting his Ph.D., Ginny remembered. Perhaps Liz was as well.

"But they don't go to school now," Ginny said. "Not while they're here at the farm."

Daisy stopped then and erupted into sobs again, burying her face in her hands. "I'm her lovey-dovey," she said. "I want to go home."

Out of nowhere tears stung Ginny's eyes. Stooping down to eye level, she gazed at the sobbing child. "Me too," Ginny said. "I miss my lovey-dovey too, and I want to go home."

Then she gave her a big, wet, muddy squeeze. "Girl hug!" she said.

Chapter 5

*E*XACTLY SIX DAYS after her arrival at the Iron Age farm, as calculated by Ginny on her log calendar, Maurice made his return. He strolled into the compound accompanied by his frog-eyed assistant, Roger, and carrying a large array of camera and video equipment. It was to be one of his regular visits, and he would spend the day interviewing the participants, photographing anything of note, and videotaping everything.

Ginny had been counting the days until his arrival not because she really wanted to see him but because he would be bringing her mail.

All morning she found herself glancing up the path for a sight of him. Fortunately she was in a good position to spot his approach, being stationed on a log outside the roundhouse in her new role as Mark's apprentice.

Ginny had finally accepted the wisdom of Karen's suggestion that she find something to do. Though Ginny had no training like the others, and though she didn't expect to be there all that long—still, it was a bit like sitting in the dentist's office: You couldn't just stare at the wall. You at least had to pick up a magazine.

With haymaking over and the harvest not yet begun, there was a lull of several weeks, a good chance for her to settle in. "Give your dad a hand with the forge," Karen had suggested.

Ginny had swallowed her pride and spent the day with her dad as he went about his tasks. He completed his tunnel and mounted his anvil on a large stump. Now all that remained to get his forge going was to make the charcoal he would burn in it.

Ginny had never stopped to wonder where charcoal came from or even what it was; it just came in a bag from the store. You dumped it into the grill, added lighter fluid, and had a cookout. But no, it turned out that long before the invention of backyard grills people had used charcoal. Making it was in fact an ancient craft practiced by an exotic and solitary breed of men, the charcoal burners, who had lived in the English forests since time immemorial.

Of course nowadays charcoal was made in factories. But as an Iron Age blacksmith Hugh would have to make his the old-fashioned way, by burning weathered oak slowly in a closed pit for many days.

He patiently explained all this to Ginny, as though she were in school and this were the lesson. He talked about incomplete combustion and sketched out the pit clamp, as it was called, with a stick in the dirt. Then he set to work digging the pit.

"Is there another shovel?" Ginny finally asked. "I could help."

He looked up distractedly. "No," he said. Then, after thinking for a moment, he added, "There is a pick. But I'm afraid we'd just chop each other's toes off."

"Then what can I do?"

"Well, this is actually a one-man job. But once we get things going, you could work the bellows. I promised Sam he could do it, but I'm sure he'll understand."

"No, that's okay," Ginny had said. "I don't want to work the bellows anyway."

Ginny had wandered around the compound for a while, feeling annoyed. One of the hens waddled across her path, and she felt a sudden urge to send it flying over the fence like a football. It took her a long time to calm down.

Eventually she settled on helping Mark make pots, partly because she liked Mark but also because she had taken a pottery class one summer and had been good at it. Of course it hadn't been Iron Age pottery. They had had a potter's wheel and glazes and an electric kiln. The clay had come from the craft supply store, packaged and ready to go.

Ginny now sat beside Mark, wedging a lump of orange clay. The motion was a lot like kneading bread—folding and squeezing—but harder on her hands. The grog—the pieces of flint and crushed limestone she was working into the clay to help it withstand the intense heat of firing— scraped the bony parts of her fingers. She was tempted to stop wedging and move on to making her pot, which was the fun part. But she knew that if the grog wasn't spread evenly throughout the clay, her pot would break.

This was actually a serious matter, because clay pots were what they used to cook in, and they had turned out to be very unreliable. Lots of beautiful pots, which had taken Mark hours and hours to make, had shattered to bits in the firing. What was worse, the ones that survived and seemed all right had a nasty habit of falling to pieces while being used, say, to cook stew. You could usually tell this had happened when you heard a string of profanity coming out of the roundhouse.

Mark was quite self-effacing about his failure. "It proves the last-name theory invalid anyway," he said.

"The what?" asked Ginny.

Mark chuckled. "I thought that since my last name is Potter, I might have some inborn talent. Descended from a long line of potters and all that," he said. "Obviously not the case. I wonder if Maurice would be interested in doing a paper on it."

It seemed clear from his expression that Mark wasn't serious.

"Do you really think you came from a family of potters?" Ginny asked after a while.

"Yes. That's where the name comes from," he said.

"Like Baker?"

"Yup. Way back when, ordinary people didn't have last names, you know, the way we do now. They just had a first name and some sort of description—like John, Robert's son."

"John Robertson!" cried Ginny.

"There you are! Or Thompson, or Jackson, or Johnson, or Williamson."

"Didn't mothers count?"

"No, I'm afraid not. Ever heard of names like Catherineson or Maryson?"

"Bummer," Ginny said.

She thought about it as she worked, making a mental list. "Weaver, Carpenter, Gardener, Shepherd, Smith—" She looked up and saw Maurice and leaped to her feet. "Mail!" she said.

There were two letters, a fat one from her mother and a thin one with flowers on the envelope from Andrea. Having tucked them delicately under her arm, Ginny carefully washed her hands.

"You want writing materials?" Maurice called to her.

"What?" asked Ginny.

"To write back." He held out several sheets of paper, some envelopes, and a ballpoint pen. Ginny ran over and retrieved them.

"Did my mother call?" she asked. "Were there any messages?"

"Oh, yes," he said, handing out mail as the others gathered around. "Just that her surgery went fine."

"That's it? Nothing about when I should come back?"

"No," said Maurice, "but I didn't actually take the call. My secretary did. Anyway, that was the message as far as I know."

Ginny turned away, exasperated, and looked for a private place to read her letters. She walked out toward the meadow, then beyond it to the edge of the woods. She found a grassy spot under a tree and settled herself there.

Hi, sweetie! Ginny read. *I miss you so much, precious child!*
Ginny could picture Rena, her arms wide, inviting her in for a hug. She did that a lot, sometimes right out of the blue. Ginny would say something perfectly unremarkable, and it would set Rena off, needing to give her a squeeze. It was weird, but Ginny liked it, and she thought it was especially cool that her mom could send a hug through the mail.

Rena went on,

> *Oh, my dear Ginny, ever since you left, I've just been thinking and thinking about all the things I should have said (or shouldn't have said)—well, you know how that goes. Anyway, bear with me (and my awful handwriting—I'm still pretty tender, can't seem to find a comfortable position to write), 'cause I need to tell you some things.*
>
> *First off, the surgery went fine—there were no complications. I do feel pretty washed out right now, but not terrible. Unfortunately, though, sweetie, they found cancer cells in quite a few of the lymph nodes. That means I'm going to have to have some further treatments, which will make me feel a lot worse. So you and I are just going to have to hang in there for a while and get through this. I am meeting with a specialist this afternoon to discuss the*

options. I'll let you know what he says, though I'd really rather you tried not to worry about me. We've each got our work to do—mine is to get well, and yours is to get to know your dad. (Stop rolling your eyes!!!)

Ginny laughed when she read that. She really had been rolling her eyes. Maybe she needed to find a more original way of showing her irritation.

I know perfectly well how you feel about your father. And yes, he does come across as kind of remote, and no, he definitely hasn't been there for you thus far. But that's not entirely his fault, Ginny—he would have been there if I had encouraged him to. It isn't fair for you to think he just didn't care.

You know, the fact that we live so far apart made a good excuse for both of us. You were so little when we divorced, and Hugh, well, I think he sort of didn't know what to do with a two-year-old all by himself. He's so quiet and turned in on himself—which drove me crazy, as I'm sure you can imagine—he just didn't know how to form a bond with you, I guess. It would have been different if we had stayed married, though. He's a truly good man, Ginny—and whether he knows it or not, he needs you as much as you need him.

Now here's the part I've been fretting about—I'm afraid my own selfishness plays a rather large part in this story. The bald truth is I wanted you all to myself. I didn't want to have to argue with Hugh over whether you went to a private school or public school, whether you studied piano or karate, how late you could stay up on school nights, all that stuff. And I'm sure it goes a whole lot deeper than I really want to follow it right now, wanting to run things, wanting all your love. (Ick, ugh! Save it for the psychiatrist!)

In my defense, dear heart, I think I hoped you'd have the same kind of sweet childhood I had, even though I just had my father, after Mother died. I never did understand why people spoke in those hushed tones back then about "single-parent households." I was the happiest kid I knew. And plenty of my friends, who had two parents, were absolutely driven 'round the bend by their bickering.

So that's why I was so sure I could make this perfect life for you. Unfortunately it seems I didn't really think it through. I never considered how chancy it was to let you depend on me—and only me—so completely. And now look what's happened. . . .

Ginny laid the letter down. What was her mother saying? That she was going to die? Ginny suddenly felt really panicked for the first time. It hadn't seemed possible before—that her mother might actually just stop being. The more she thought about it, the more frightened she became. She put her face in her hands and cried.

After a while, when she had let it all out, Ginny lay back in the grass, the speckles of sunlight filtering through the leaves overhead warming her flushed cheeks. She listened, comforted by the tranquil sounds of outdoors: the chatter of squirrels; birds singing; wind blowing through the barley field; now and then, from far away, the sound of someone's voice. Then she heard the soft brushing of bare feet in the grass.

"Are you all right?" It was Corey.

Ginny wiped her cheeks and sat up. "I guess," she said.

"A letter from your mum?" he asked, sitting down beside her. She thought he might at least have asked if she minded.

"Yes," she said.

"Bad news?"

"Who knows!" Ginny spit out in exasperation, waving the letter around. "Grown-ups write this stuff—like, you can't figure out what they're saying!"

"Did she tell you when she wants you to come home?"

"I don't know. I haven't finished it."

"Then finish it."

Ginny picked up the letter and continued reading. There wasn't a whole lot more. Sophie was fine—no puppies yet. Andrea had asked for Ginny's address and would be writing soon. Rena closed with kisses and one last sermon on the hidden virtues of Hugh Dorris.

"Well?" said Corey when she put the letter down.

"If she thinks he's so great, why did she divorce him?" she muttered.

"Your dad?"

"Yeah," she said. "Nothing about when I can come back and lots about how it's not my dad's fault that he ignored me for the last thirteen years."

"You're not much like him," Corey observed flatly.

"Yeah?" Ginny looked up at him with interest. "Since I got here, everybody keeps saying how much we look alike. I think I look like my mom."

"No." Corey corrected her. "You do look like your dad. But you're not like him as a person. Stuck-up, I mean."

"He's not stuck-up," Ginny countered.

"With people like me, he is."

"What do you mean, *people like you?*"

"I mean, working class."

"Corey, that's stupid! My dad works."

"Yeah, he works, Ginny, but he's not working class," he said. "You're American. You wouldn't understand."

"Well, if you're talking about prejudice," Ginny said sarcastically, "I guess you're right. I wouldn't know about that because everybody's rich in America and everybody gets treated the same. . . . Don't you ever go to the movies?"

"Forget it," Corey said. "It's not important. I just meant I think your dad's a bit of a cold fish, but you're not like that at all. You're really nice."

Ginny blushed. "Well, you must be wrong about my dad," she said, laughing, "because it says right here"—(and she picked up her mother's letter)—"it says he's 'bright, funny, and sweet' and that if I can coax him out of himself, I will discover that he 'loves generously.'"

They both lay back in the grass for a while and listened to the sounds of summer.

"Do you like it here?" Ginny finally asked.

"Not much," he said. "I actually walked out a week after we got here."

"Really?" Ginny sat up.

"Yeah, I got as far as the road, and I stood there in this stupid getup with my thumb out. And one car passed, and the guy turned around and stared at me and kept on going. Then I came to my senses and hiked back."

"But you didn't have to come here like I did. I mean, my mom literally put me on a plane and said, 'Go!'"

"Well, in a manner of speaking, I did."

"What do you mean?"

"Maybe I'll tell you about it sometime," he said, and, putting his hand gently on her shoulder, got to his feet. "I'll leave you to answer your letter in peace. I've got to go write my girlfriend," he added, "and convince her I'm worth waiting for." He waggled his eyebrows expressively, then turned to go.

"Thanks for cheering me up," Ginny called to his back.

He waved without turning, striding along purposefully on his long legs, in that stiff-hipped way only boys walk. Then he turned and called, "Just tell her you want to come home. Just say it."

Ginny handed her letters to Maurice, who was preoccupied with interviewing Mark and merely slipped them into his briefcase without a glance. Ginny couldn't shake the feeling that she was handing in a homework assignment, one she had completed with special care. She felt somehow that her letters should be acknowledged.

Her answer to Andrea had been lighthearted, in keeping with the incredulous "you've gone *where*?" tone of Andrea's letter, which featured much underlining and lots of exclamation marks. Ginny made it all sound like an adventure, corrected the impression that she was living like a "caveman," and threw in a juicy description of Corey (leaving out the girlfriend) to make Andrea jealous. She finished with assurances that she would be there for the first day of school, with a great tan and full of stories.

The letter to her mom had been harder, especially since she was used to writing on a computer, where you could delete anything you didn't like.

It felt strange to be the one comforting her mom, and it sounded so lame to say, "I know you'll be just fine." Also, while she wanted to make her case for hurrying home, she didn't want to sound whiny either. In the end she said what she perceived to be all the right things, including assurances that she and her dad were getting along famously. Mission accomplished, it said between the lines, now bring me home.

She ended it with "See you soon!" It was thirty-one days till school started.

"When do you come back next?" Ginny asked Maurice, interrupting his interview.

He turned to look at her pointedly. "August first," he said dryly. It was as though she had asked him what color underwear he had on.

"He has to be here to record the lunacy of Lugnasa," Mark said, grinning.

"The what?" Ginny asked.

"It's a Celtic festival," said Mark. "Sort of an early harvest celebration. First fruits and all that."

Maurice switched off the video camera with mild exasperation. Mark was obviously bent on talking about the upcoming festivities, and Maurice would have to wait till he was done before he could continue documenting the failure of the Iron Age pottery works.

"Like Thanksgiving?" Ginny asked.

"Same idea, anyway, though your Thanksgiving is a new thing, relatively speaking. Commemorating a meal with the Indians or something, isn't it? But some of our holidays, even religious ones, were once very ancient pagan festivals."

"Like what?"

"Well, there's Beltain, on May first. It became May Day. And Samain on October thirty-first—Allhallows' Eve."

"Halloween! Really? That was an ancient—what did you call it?—Celtic festival?"

Maurice couldn't restrain himself. He threw up his hands in disgust, got to his feet, and headed for the lavatory.

"Don't mind him," said Mark.

"What was that all about?"

"Probably it was because you didn't know what 'Celtic' means."

"Is that some terrible sin?"

"No, of course not. It's just really basic. Like showing up at school and picking up a book and saying, 'What's this?'"

"So tell me before he gets back," said Ginny.

"The Celts are a people, Ginny, the Britons of the Iron

Age. They're who we're pretending to be. So we decided to celebrate their festivals, for fun really, but also just to get a sense of the flow of a year in their world."

"Oh," said Ginny.

"Most of the people in Ireland and Scotland are Celtic. I guess there are a lot in the U.S. too."

Maurice strolled back, somewhat more under control. He sat back down on the log, cradled the video camera in his hands, checked to see that the battery was turned off, and launched into a lecture.

"The Celtic year was divided into two seasons," he said, "the cold and the warm. The cold season begins with the festival of Samain, on October thirty-first. The warm season begins with Beltain on May first."

"The year is divided into quarters by two other big holidays, each falling right in the middle of a season. So on February first, halfway through the cold season, there was Imbolc, a day of purification. The middle festival of the warm season is Lugnasa, which is the one we will be celebrating in about two weeks."

He lifted his eyebrows as if to say, Got it? Ginny responded with a silent nod. Then, just to irritate him—because she could just as easily have asked Mark later—she added, "What will we be doing to celebrate Lugnasa exactly?"

Maurice took a deep breath. "In keeping with Celtic tradition there will be a big feast and lots of games. There will not be any human sacrifices, however, as was probably also traditional." He paused, then added, "Though it's tempting."

Ginny returned to wedging her clay. Maurice turned the video camera back on, pointed it at Mark, and resumed the interview.

"What, in your opinion, is the most likely reason the pots continue to fail? Do you think it's the kiln?"

"No, I really don't," Mark said into the camera, "though I'd still rather we were firing the pots in a pit clamp, which I consider more authentic."

Maurice waved a hand dismissively. "That's just Howard being pedantic," he said. "There's firm evidence for kilns from Danish peat bogs."

"Yes, but as Howard is so fond of saying, 'This ain't Denmark, now, is it?'"

"Who's Howard?" Ginny asked. Maurice paused the video camera and sighed.

"An expert on Iron Age pottery," he said. "One of our consultants." He waited pointedly for further questions. When there weren't any, he resumed filming.

"The question is," he said to Mark, "is the firing inadequate?"

"Well, who knows?" said Mark, shrugging. "But my gut instinct says that the problem is the clay."

"Nonsense," said Maurice, glancing at the small mountain of red clay that had been dumped at the site. "It's commercial potter's clay. It's excellent."

"I'm sure it is," said Mark, "but it's very pure. I'd guess we're not working enough grog into it."

"All right, then, thanks," Maurice said abruptly, getting

up and switching off the video camera again. He looked about for another subject, spotted Faith and Millie leading a couple of the goats in to be milked, and headed in their direction.

"I don't guess he wants to interview me," Ginny remarked, grinning.

"Next time," Mark said, grinning back.

Dinner that night was quieter than usual. Maybe, Ginny thought, they all were thinking about the people they'd left behind.

Already she was regretting that she hadn't said more interesting things in her letter. She should have told her mom what it was like here, eating dinner outside in the twilight with the occasional hen dashing up and making a dive for your bread. It would have amused her to picture Ginny eating stew with her fingers, to imagine all the slurping and licking of bowls. Ginny could have wittily observed that she now knew why table manners were such an important part of modern etiquette. Once people started using forks and spoons and napkins, they wanted to put as much distance as possible between themselves and those unfortunate peasants who were still picking up meat with their fingers and throwing the bones to the dogs.

She should have told Rena about poor little freaked-out Daisy and how she'd rescued her in the rainstorm. And Corey of the beautiful skin and blue eyes who thought her dad was stuck-up. That Hugh was building an Iron Age forge but wouldn't let her help. And how she became the

75

potter's apprentice and what a lot of work it was to prepare the clay before you even began to make the pot. She could have described her first attempt to build a coil pot and how spectacularly it had collapsed into something more like a place mat than anything else. Next time she would write all that. She would make her next letter really interesting and funny.

That night Ginny woke with a start. She had been having the house dream again, the one where she had moved into an enormous mansion. It had room after room, all of them huge with high ceilings and every one of them cavernously empty. They became a sort of maze, so that she couldn't find her way out. She was always alone in there.

Ginny wormed her way out of her sheepskin cocoon and sat up. A dim glow penetrated the inner wall of the little room. It was from the all-nighter, the large, fresh-cut log that burned slowly until dawn, when the cook would bring in fresh kindling and get it going again for breakfast.

Ginny needed to use the lavatory and reflected for the hundredth time that modern bathrooms were probably the greatest achievement of the modern era. She considered crawling back under the covers and waiting till morning but knew she would not sleep comfortably if she did. She'd dream of toilets probably. She got up and walked quietly into the main part of the roundhouse.

Ginny stood beside the hearth for a minute, listening to the sleeping sounds around her. Flora, from her accustomed place by the fire, looked up dreamily, then put her head back down and closed her eyes. Ginny stepped softly out-side. It was a balmy night, the breeze fresh and damp against her face. The smell of smoke and animals hung in the air.

On her way back Ginny stopped for a moment to look up. The moon had already set, and the sky was a dazzling mass of stars. The sight of them both thrilled and terrified her. Once, a few years before, Ginny had lain in bed think-ing about the vastness of space. She had pictured herself soaring through the night sky, past millions of stars and on and on toward the point where there was nothing left but blackness and empty space. It had chilled her to the bone, and she had started to cry. Since then she had magnified this terror by imagining a time when the world would have ended and that vast, cold universe would just go on spin-ning its empty planets for all time. Everything she had ever known would be gone, gone for always, and no conscious-ness would remain to remember it.

Ginny shivered and looked away from the stars, back to the comfort of the small compound with its tidy little fence, which sat on a big, solid island with a real shore around it. And all of it sat on a planet where the land met the sky in neat and predictable ways. The shadowy bulk of the round-house waited at the end of the path, black against the soft glow of the hillside. It made her feel safe.

Inside she slipped between the sheepskins and wiggled around till she got comfortable. From the top bunk she could hear her father's soft, rhythmic breathing.

She closed her eyes. Apple, banana, cheese, she thought.

Doughnuts, eggs, french fries, grapes. It was her going-to-sleep alphabet game. Sometimes she grouped the As and Bs together, then the Cs and Ds. Ambitious bear. Cute dog. Eager fox. Sometimes she did names. Abigail Brown. Corey Donnelley. Eventually and always, just like this night, Ginny would fall asleep.

Chapter 6

THE FOLLOWING MORNING brought a nasty surprise. Shortly after breakfast Ian discovered that a hiveful of bees had escaped. Or, to be more precise, they were swarming—something bees did naturally whenever they were unhappy for some reason.

With the queen in the lead, they had streamed out of the little wattle-and-daub hive and buzzed around aimlessly for about forty minutes until the queen had come to rest on one of the top branches of an ash tree just outside the compound. The other bees had joined her there, piling one on top of the other in a melon-size cluster. There they would stay until messenger bees, scouting for a better location, came to give them directions. Then they would fly off again to establish a new hive elsewhere.

The village beekeepers, Ian and Bennett, were perplexed. They didn't really know why the bees had decided to swarm, beyond some kind of general bee dissatisfaction. By the time Ginny arrived, the whole village had crowded around to hear them discuss it.

"Maybe it's just the hives they don't like," Bennett said. "They're rather primitive, you know, and quite a bit of the daub has flaked off. They'd be awfully damp and drafty inside, don't you think?"

"Well, maybe," said Ian doubtfully, "but, you know, modern beekeepers have this happen sometimes too. I think it's probably the weather or the amount of nectar in the flowers—some fool thing like that."

Ginny spotted her dad leaning against the storehouse, his arms crossed and a slightly worried expression on his face. There was something unfriendly and perverse about the way he always stood just a little apart from everybody else. Maybe Corey was right; maybe he did feel superior. Ginny walked over and stood beside him.

"Does this mean we won't have any more honey?" she asked.

"No," he said, "though it will cut down on our harvest if we can't get the bees back. Plus, it would be a shame to lose them."

"Get the bees back?" Ginny looked perplexed.

"Come look," said Hugh, leading her over to the fence and pointing across the clearing to the top of a nearby tree. "See that big lump, way up on a high branch?" Ginny scanned the treetops for a moment, squinting. Then she saw it, dark and glistening. "That's the whole cluster of bees," Hugh said. "They won't stay there all that long— maybe for a day. So we've got a little time yet to try to recapture them. It's called taking the swarm."

"How on earth?" Ginny asked.

"Well, according to Ian, you're supposed to get a spare hive ready, then go fetch the swarm—ever so carefully—and lay it out on a clean white cloth in front of the entrance to the hive. Then you just sort of invite them back in."

"You're kidding, right?"

"Actually, no. I'll admit it sounds bizarre, but apparently it's done all the time. Of course you usually wear gloves and veils so as not to get stung."

"But how do you pick them up?" Ginny asked, still not able to picture it.

"You break off the branch. In theory the bees stay attached, and you can carry them right over to the new hive very handily."

Ginny looked at the swarm again and saw that it would be no easy task to get up there, let alone climb back down with a branch full of bees in one hand.

"It looks dangerous to me," she said.

"Yes," Hugh admitted, "I was thinking the same thing. I'm not sure the bees are worth it."

The group was breaking up now, Ian and Bennett having worked out their strategy and everyone else running off to get the necessary equipment. The first order of business was to make some quick repairs on one of the spare hives, then set it up on a low platform with a cloak draped in front. The cloth was neither clean nor white, but it would have to do.

Liz and Tom fetched a ladder they had made while build-

ing the roundhouse. Daisy trailed along beside them, clinging on to the ladder and making it harder for them to carry.
Millie got one of the big baskets used for hauling hay and
attached a long rope to it.

"What's that for?" Ginny asked.

"A sort of bee elevator," she said brightly. "Ian thought it
would be a safer way to get them down. One person breaks
off the branch, while another is right below with the basket
to catch them. Then cover 'em up with a cloth, and lower
the whole thing down with a rope."

"That's pretty good," Hugh said. "Excellent, in fact.
Who's going up the tree?"

"Bennett and Ian," said Millie. When Hugh made a face,
she said defensively, "Well, they are the beekeepers."

Neither of them seemed like a tree climber to Ginny. Ian
was too short, and Bennett was too clumsy. "Nat volun-
teered," Millie added, raising her dark eyebrows in amuse-
ment, "but Jonas put a quash on that."

"I should hope!" said Hugh, horrified.

Ginny thought this ironic. Grown-ups just assumed they
could do things better than children could. Yet she had no
doubt that nine-year-old Nat was the best tree climber in
the village.

The group began heading off in the direction of the bee
tree, carrying the ladder and the basket. It wasn't far, actually—just on the edge of the clearing. But once there,
looking up, Ginny was sickened by the height. The bottom
branches were above the tallest person's reach; hence the
ladder.

Bennett began his climb, and it was instantly obvious to Ginny that he had never done such a thing in his life. At home he probably let Faith change the lightbulbs. It was a good thing Mark was holding the ladder, because it wobbled alarmingly from side to side against the trunk.

"He's going to kill himself," Ginny whispered. Hugh didn't answer, but he looked anxious.

Bennett hoisted himself awkwardly onto the lowest branch. He dangled there, like a tipsy spider, unsure how to get himself upright and in a position to go higher. As he thrashed about, to the amused giggles of Nat and Sam, Ginny noticed that he was edging himself out too far, and the branch was beginning to bend. Before she could warn him, Bennett uttered a gasp of surprise, and with the fluid motion of a toddler on his first time down a slide, he slipped off the branch and plummeted to the ground. He landed on his back with a horrible thud.

For a few seconds he couldn't catch his breath. Then he gulped in air convulsively and let out a moan.

Faith hurried to his side and knelt there, agitated and confused, gripping Bennett's hand and weeping. She was never at her best in a crisis, being rather high-strung by nature, and she seemed especially helpless and ineffectual now.

Karen moved in to assess the damage and calmed Faith with brisk assurances. She saw that Bennett's left shoulder had hit a rock hard and was bleeding. His arms and hands were scraped and bloody, too, but nothing seemed to be broken.

"Bennett," Karen said, "do you know where you are?"

He looked up at the tree above him. "In the woods?" he said, sounding a little surprised.

"That's right, and do you know why you're lying here?"

He looked around for clues. "Um, no. Not exactly." His voice seemed a little slurred.

Daisy was whimpering loudly and clinging to her mother's skirts. Karen asked her, somewhat irritably, to cut it out.

Karen went on asking questions for a few more minutes, then patted his shoulder gently, turning to Faith. "I think he's fine," she said. "It's nothing worse than a mild concussion, though we ought to keep a close eye on him for the next few hours. Will you let me know if you notice any sign of confusion or headache, vision changes—things like that?" Faith nodded gravely.

Ian helped Bennett to his feet and led him to a grassy spot out of harm's way. "Don't want me landing on your head, now do you, if I go falling out of that blasted tree too?" he joked.

"Oh, Ian," Faith said, "don't you dare!"

"Actually," Corey said, his hand up like he was asking to be called on in class, "Can I do it? I'd like to go up and get the branch down—if you don't mind, Ian. You could come up below with the basket." Ginny thought Corey had the air of a knight going into battle to restore the family honor.

Ian shrugged. "Fine with me," he said. "Whatever."

Corey headed straight for the ladder and began climbing with confidence and ease. At least he knows what he's doing, Ginny thought. When he reached the fateful branch, he merely grasped it near the trunk and, thus steadied, continued to the top rung of the ladder. From there he got a second handhold and began the delicate procedure of working himself up, from branch to branch, toward the top of the tree.

Now Ian started up after him, a rope tied to his waist and trailing after him like a long tail. This was to haul up the basket once he was in place below Corey and to lower it again afterward, full of bees.

The two men made their way cautiously up to their positions. Now it became apparent that the branch containing the bees was far too slender to bear Corey's weight. Even the mass of bees was bending it down. Corey worked out a strategy of standing on the crotch of a lower branch, clutching the trunk with one hand, and leaning out to break off the far end of the limb bearing the bees. Ginny could imagine how hard that would be. Green wood bends rather than breaks. To break a sizable branch with only one hand, while balancing on a narrow limb, would be nearly impossible. Corey struggled away, accomplishing little more than to swish the branch around and annoy the bees. About a dozen of them broke off from the clump and buzzed angrily around his head.

"I need two hands for this," he called down.

"I don't think you could fit another person up there," Hugh shouted back.

"I know," said Corey. "I'm going to try something different." He scooted up higher in the tree, which now began to lean alarmingly. Holding on only with his legs, he reached down and, with both hands, worked on the branch. He bent it slowly downward, almost straight down. There was a splitting sound, and timid cheers went up from below.

"It's not broken clean through," he said. "There's some fibrous stuff that just won't give way." He let go with one hand and began fumbling in his pouch for something to cut it with.

"Oh, no!" Millie exclaimed, burying her head in her hands.

"Corey, please be careful," Faith pleaded.

Now Corey was sawing away at the branch with a flint. The motion caused the whole tree to shake and more bees to separate from the swarm. They were hovering around Ian now too, but he couldn't brush them away. He needed one hand to hang on and the other to hold the basket.

Suddenly the last of the branch gave way with a vicious jerk, and for a moment Corey held it still, more or less above the basket. "Ready?" he asked Ian in a throaty voice.

"Yes," Ian answered. He was more than ready to get down.

"Oh, help!" cried Corey, slipping. Quickly he let go of the bees and grabbed the nearest branch, scrambling for a solid handhold.

As it fell, the branch struck the side of the basket, dislodging a shower of comatose bees, which rained down on the people below. Frantically everyone began screaming and brushing bees out of their hair and clothing. Only desperate crashing and moaning from above reminded them that the drama still went on. Ian was now hanging by his arms, both feet dangling free. Corey was upside down, his legs entwined in the branches and one hand grasping the basket. The rope, now attached to the basket, hung uselessly down. A feeling of helpless hysteria fell over the group below.

"Move back," Hugh said to the crowd. "Get out of the way." Then to Ian and Corey: "Drop the blasted thing if you have to. Just whatever you do, don't fall!"

Ginny thought Ian seemed okay. He was strong and appeared to have regained his composure. Deliberately he pulled himself back to a sitting position. Then, taking firm hold of a nearby branch to steady himself, he retrieved the rope. He tied one end to the branch, then reached out again, this time for the basket. Cautiously he began lowering it to the ground. The cover had fallen out of the tree, but Jonas had it ready to throw over the bees when it reached bottom.

Free of the basket, Corey gripped the trunk and hung there, partially hidden in the leaves. From below they could hear him breathing hard. "You start down first," he told Ian.

"I'm going to drop the rope!" Ian called down. Jonas pulled the covered basket out of the way and stood back as the rope came tumbling down. Then Ian began his descent. He did it cautiously but with dispatch. When he reached the last branch, he ignored the ladder and, with a Tarzan swing, dropped down, bending his knees to cushion the impact. There were bee stings on his hands and one or two on his face. Millie pulled him over into the sunlight so she could see to remove the stingers.

Only when Ian was free and clear did Corey begin rearranging his position in the tree. He seemed to take forever, moving from branch to branch, stopping often to rest.

"Are you all right?" Faith shouted up to him nervously.

"I'm all right," he assured her, but his voice sounded strange. He continued his slow climb down.

"I think he's hurt," said Millie.

"Do you need help?" Ian shouted.

There was a pause, rather too long. "No," said Corey, and he came farther down. Only then could they see his face. It was covered with angry blisters; his eyes were almost swollen shut.

"Oh, no! Oh, poor Corey!" Faith whispered frantically. He was feeling his way down, blind.

"I'm going up there," said Mark.

"I'm not sure you should," said Hugh softly. "He seems to know what he's doing. If we get you up there too, you might make things worse."

They watched helplessly. "Can you see at all, Corey?" asked Mark.

"No," he said.

"The next branch is a little to the left of your foot," Mark told him. "That's it. It looks solid. Hold steady, and see if it will bear your weight."

It did. Corey made it down another level. Slowly, carefully, Mark talked him down. "Now about forty degrees to your right."

"I can't," said Corey hoarsely.

"It's not far," Mark urged. "Just down and to the right."

"I can't use my right foot," Corey said leadenly.

"Oh, great!" muttered Mark grimly.

Flora, who had been watching all this with cool detachment, now decided to bark furiously.

Mark stamped his foot to drive her off. She retreated about halfway to the gate, then sat down and barked again.

Mark stood there for a minute, biting his lip in concentration. Then he started up. Nobody stopped him; Corey was far enough down in the tree now for two climbers. Gently Mark urged him down, supporting him in the awkward places. Corey's upper body strength allowed him to do much of the work with his arms, but he was clearly not himself. He was in a lot of pain.

The ladder was trickiest of all. Corey had to hold on with his hands while lowering his left leg from rung to rung. When he was low enough, Jonas lifted him off and, with Liz's help, laid him gently on a soft pile of leaves.

Karen had run for her doctor's bag and a bucket of water. Now she knelt by Corey's face and studied the situation. "Corey," she said urgently, "how's your breathing?"

"Okay," he said hoarsely.

"I need to look at your throat," she said very slowly, as if to a small child. "Just to make sure." She had a small, flat piece of wood in her hand. Ginny recognized it at once as a homemade tongue depressor. "Say ahh," Karen said, pressing on his tongue and turning his head slightly so she could see better. "Looks pretty good," she said. "You're not allergic to bee stings, are you?"

Corey shook his head slowly.

"Excellent," said Karen. "I think you'll be fine. Now just

lie still." With a small, sharp flint, she began gently teasing the stingers out of Corey's face and washing the red welts with a wet cloth.

Corey looked hideous, his handsome face a mass of scarlet lumps, grossly swollen. His arms were badly stung, too.

Nat and Sam scurried over for a look. "Ooo, gross!" Sam said.

"Will you get out of the way?" shouted Jonas irritably, jerking his boys back with a look of thunder on his face.

Faith was sobbing hysterically now. Hugh guided her over to where Bennett was resting and made her sit beside him. "Stop it, Faith," he whispered firmly. "This isn't helping. He'll be all right."

Faith's sobbing had a bad effect on Daisy, who now grew increasingly upset. It was putting everybody on edge.

"Ginny," Liz said, "would you mind taking Daisy back to the compound?"

Ginny was stunned. "No, I want to stay here and help," she said. She didn't have the nerve to look right at Liz while she said it, though. Out of the corner of her eye she saw Liz pick up the wailing child and stride away.

Ginny scooted in to help Karen look for stingers. "Don't pull them, Ginny," Karen said. "Scrape them out. With your fingernail or"—Karen glanced at Ginny's hands, the nails bitten to the quick—"or find a flint." The leaves and branches of the tree had brushed off most of the stingers in Corey's arms. Still, Ginny found quite a few and did her best to tease them out gently as Karen was doing. She didn't have a cloth, so she dribbled water on his arm and spread it over the blisters gently with her fingers. Hugh sat down opposite Ginny and worked on the other arm.

Leaving the wet cloth draped over Corey's eyes, Karen moved around to check his foot. She probed carefully for several minutes, asking him to tell her where it hurt. "It may be broken, but I don't think so," she told Hugh finally. "Probably a sprained ligament. Got twisted by a branch when he was doing that acrobatic thing up there." Then Karen got to her feet and called for everyone's attention. "We need to construct a stretcher of some kind," she told them.

"I think we could just carry him back to the compound," Jonas said. "Wouldn't that be faster?"

"Yes, that would be fine," said Karen, "but we still need the stretcher. I sent Tom down to the road to phone a doctor. I'd like to get Corey down there as soon as we can. Bennett, too, but I think he can walk. They both ought to be checked out in hospital."

"Wouldn't it be better to bring the ambulance up here than to carry him all that way?" Hugh asked.

"I'm afraid we don't have the keys to the gate, Hugh, so they can't drive in."

Hugh went slack-jawed. "Oh, Karen—I'm sorry! It never occurred to us. We were so worried about outsiders wandering in and interrupting us—" He looked truly abashed. Sick, almost. Impulsively Ginny took his arm and gave it a squeeze.

"Don't worry about it," Karen said briskly. "It could have been a whole lot worse. Come on, lend a hand."

Gently Hugh and Jonas lifted Corey and carried him

back to the compound, an awkward job that required them to walk sideways. Faith said she wanted to go in the ambulance with them, which Karen agreed was fine. "But you have to stay cool, Faith," she said bluntly. "You're no use to anybody if you're freaking out. Okay?"

Faith nodded and wiped her eyes.

Once everyone calmed down, the stretcher problem was easily solved. Many segments of the fences were made of individual hurdles, strong upright poles with branches of hazel woven in between them. They could easily be removed from their supports and, with a couple of stout branches tied along either side, would make an excellent stretcher. They covered the hurdle with several sheepskins, then moved Corey onto it.

Hugh, Mark and Jonas—two stretcher-bearers and an alternate—headed off toward the road, with Bennett, Faith, and Karen walking behind. For the time being, at least, almost half their number was gone.

For the rest of that day an air of anxiety hung over the compound. Though Karen tried hard to reassure everyone, the experience had been sobering.

Hugh, in particular, was extremely withdrawn. He scarcely spoke at all, to the point of rudeness. Ginny had to remind herself that he wasn't mad at her, because that's exactly what it felt like. But she was learning to read his moods and give them their proper names. This was more like despondency.

That night, as she lay in her lumpy bed, only a few feet

below her father, she heard him tossing restlessly. She wanted to say something, but somehow she was afraid to, as though he would explode with anger. In her head she said it over and over: Dad? Dad?

"Dad?" she said finally.

"What?" came his voice from overhead. He had to clear his throat, probably from not talking for so long, Ginny thought. Forgotten how to use his voice.

"What do you think of Corey?"

He didn't answer for a long time. She wondered whether he had heard her question at all. Then, finally, he said, "What do you mean?"

"I mean, do you like him?"

"He's a nice boy."

"He doesn't think you like him," she said. "Because he's working class."

"Oh, that's garbage," Hugh said angrily. "Ridiculous!"

"That's what I told him," Ginny answered.

There was another long silence. Ginny tried again. "He's going to be okay, isn't he?"

"Yes, he is."

"You seem kind of upset," she went on, timidly. This was like creeping up on a bear.

Hugh gave a bitter snort.

"Are you? Upset?" This was really hard!

"Yes," he said, still sounding angry. "Of course I'm upset! We should have left the bees alone in the first place. It was far too risky. I should never, ever have let Corey go up that tree. And then, icing on the cake, there are no keys to unlock the gate, so we had to drag poor Bennett and Corey all the way down to the road. Unbelievable!"

"Yeah," Ginny said lamely. "We all make mistakes." Great, she thought. Really deep advice. Very profound.

After a while he said, "We certainly do." But he sounded calmer.

Ginny closed her eyes and tried to relax. Ace bandages, candy dispenser, eager fools, gorgeous hat . . .

"Dad?"

"What, Ginny?"

"Whatever happened to the bees?"

"They came to their senses," he said. "They're back home, all snug in their beds."

"Oh, good," she said. Then, softly: "I wish everybody was."

Chapter 7

BENNETT RETURNED THE next afternoon. He just walked into the compound, accompanied by Maurice. Though he hadn't had a haircut or a shave, he was noticeably cleaner than before. He had shampooed his hair and combed it too. There was a distinct floral smell about him, most likely from the soap. Aside from that, though, he was pretty much the same. The doctor had treated his shoulder wound and run some X rays but hadn't admitted him to the hospital. Bennett had survived his fall with remarkably little damage. He had suffered a minor concussion, just as Karen suspected, but was recovering nicely. The main concern now was to make sure he didn't hit his head again anytime soon. A repeat injury could prove far more dangerous than the first one, perhaps even fatal.

Bennett said Corey was fine but still pretty uncomfortable from the bee stings. Faith had decided to stay on and look after him. She would bring him back soon, probably in a day or two.

An expression of immense relief on his face, Hugh shook Bennett's hand vigorously, as if to congratulate him on winning the Nobel Prize. Maurice smiled benignly on, chin upraised, eyes half-closed, like a big seal at the zoo, posing on a rock.

Ginny sidled over to where they were standing. Though she knew she shouldn't interrupt, she had to ask. Any messages? Any letters?

But Hugh got to Maurice first. "We need a key to the gate," he said. "You know, we couldn't get an ambulance in here because it was locked."

"Relax," said Maurice. "I heard all about it from Karen." He dug into the pocket of his trousers and pulled out a key. He pressed it into Hugh's hand, covering it with his own for a few seconds, in a gesture of patient consolation.

He can't help it, Ginny thought. He just has a basically bad personality. Maurice was being as obnoxious and patronizing to Hugh as he usually was to her.

"I was wondering whether we ought to have some sort of two-way radio or cellular phone out here," Hugh said, apparently missing Maurice's signals that he was being a silly boy. "Hiking down to the road and knocking on someone's door to call for help is really a bit iffy in an emergency situation."

"Come on, Hugh! You've got a bunch of healthy young people here. Nobody's going to have a heart attack. If you'll just refrain from sending people up trees in search of bees, there won't be any emergencies."

"Maurice, I beg to differ," said Hugh heatedly.

"Someone could get kicked in the face while milking a cow. Someone could chop off a toe with an ax. It's totally irresponsible for us to put these people in peril just because the idea of having modern equipment here fouls up our Iron Age lifestyle."

Throughout this outburst Maurice had been nervously edging Hugh away from the roundhouse, presumably so the others wouldn't hear.

"I promise not to ask for a television," Hugh added dryly.

Ginny burst into laughter. Noticing her for the first time, Hugh reached over and put his arm around her shoulder.

"All right! All right!" Maurice said, throwing up his hands. "I'll look into it."

"Is that sort of like 'It's in the mail,' Maurice?" Hugh asked, pressing.

"I'll look into it," he said again. Then, patting Hugh on the arm in a comradely manner, he turned to go.

"Maurice," Ginny called, "speaking of mail—"

"No!" he said, and left.

Having Bennett back cheered everyone's spirits. It was as though a broken link in the chain of connection had been repaired.

The villagers had begun to feel like an extended family, united by common tasks and goals. Even Ginny, who had been there such a short time, felt it. Living side by side, sharing everything, they came to know and count on one another in a way that was both intense and commonplace.

97

The effect was magnified by their isolation. Losing even one person upset the balance and their sense of security.

It upset their work schedule too. Until Corey and Faith returned, some minor adjustments would have to be made. Bunny would take Faith's regular place in the milking shed. Liz said she and Tom would take Faith and Bennett's turn in the kitchen the next day. But, she added, it would really help if someone could look after Daisy.

"It's hard to watch a five-year-old and cook for sixteen people at the same time," she said. (It was only fourteen people now, Ginny calculated, but she kept that to herself.)

Looking back later, Ginny realized she should have known this was coming. From the moment Ginny arrived, Liz had seen the word baby-sitter tattooed on her forehead. Until now it had been an occasional thing. "Oh, Daisy's lost. Ginny, would you go find her?" "Oh, Daisy's crying. Ginny, would you take her back to the compound?" But Liz had bigger plans for Ginny now. She was to be the new nanny.

It was obvious to Ginny why Liz had picked her out: She was a teenage girl. Old enough to do the job, powerless enough to be forced into it. In a final twist of the knife Liz suggested coolly that since Ginny hadn't been properly trained in any of the crafts, she wasn't really pulling her weight in the village anyway.

"I don't want to!" Ginny whispered to her dad. "Why can't Nat take care of Daisy? He does a lot less than I do around here, and he's plenty old enough." Hugh didn't seem to have heard, so Ginny poked him, agitated. He turned and studied his daughter thoughtfully, as though he had just learned something new about her, something surprising, and was trying to take it in. She found this disconcerting.

All at once it flashed through her mind that Rena must have written him a letter too. Working on this relationship from both sides! Ginny tried to remember if he had gotten any mail the other day and conjured up a vague picture of Hugh standing at the door of the roundhouse, reading something. Of course, it could have been a letter from anybody. He was sure to have friends or colleagues who would write to him.

"I know, I know," Hugh said softly, leading her away from the group so they could talk privately. "But it would be a real help to the group, you know, if you'd do it. She's driving us all bonkers, if you want to know the truth."

Ginny sighed heavily and made a face.

"Ginny, listen. Sometimes we get jobs we don't want, but we do them anyway," he went on. That was as lame as "We all make mistakes," Ginny thought, which made them even. She decided to let him get away with it.

"What about Nat?" she reminded him. "Why can't he do it?"

"You're not serious," Hugh said. "Think about it."

"Okay, bad idea," Ginny conceded. "But here's the big question. Why did Liz and Tom bother to have a child if they didn't want to take care of her? Why do they think it's somebody else's job to raise their kid?"

Hugh was silent for a long time. "That is a big question,"

he said at last. "Let's just say it's a cultural thing."

"Having nannies, you mean?"

Hugh nodded. "And boarding schools at the age of seven. Very remote parenting. Very British."

"So maybe Liz should have brought the nanny," Ginny said sourly. "I like being the potter's apprentice!"

She said it so solemnly that Hugh laughed. Then he turned serious again. "Why don't you give it a try," he said.

"You know it won't just be for tomorrow, don't you? She's going to stick me with Daisy for as long as I'm here."

"She probably will," he said, nodding repeatedly as though he were hearing inner music. "But you know, Ginny, I think you could help her. She's a sad, confused little girl."

"Yeah," Ginny said. She knew exactly how Daisy felt.

Daisy had a very ugly rag doll that she had decided to love. She suggested that she and Ginny play with it. It became apparent that what Daisy wanted to do was sit side by side on the ground while she bounced it up and down and made it talk.

I will lose my mind, Ginny thought.

"You can be the horsey," Daisy suggested.

"No, wait," Ginny said. "I have a better idea. Let's go pick berries. Then we can all have some for dessert."

"Can I bring Lulu?"

"Sure, go for it," Ginny said, finding a small basket to take with them.

"We'll be back by lunchtime," she told Liz and Tom.

Maybe it was just her imagination, but Ginny thought Liz looked absolutely radiant.

From her summers on Nantucket Ginny had learned how to find wild berries. It had always been one of her summer joys, along with crabbing and kite flying and riding bikes and walking on the beach. Dewberries grew all along the Madaket bike path, and the road to the lamp lady's house was full of blackberry bushes. Rena had devised a blackberry hook, an old cane she bought at the thrift shop. It was perfect for bringing those thorny, out-of-reach branches—always the most thickly laden with plump berries—down to where you could get at them. On a good day they could pick enough berries to make two big pies.

Rena had taught Ginny to make a lattice crust, because she said it was a shame to hide such pretty berries under a tent of pastry. They would roll out the dough, then cut it into strips with a pastry wheel. This looked to Ginny like a miniature pizza cutter, except that the wheel was wavy, giving the strips a scalloped edge. Once all the strips were cut, they laid them on top of the filling in a crisscross pattern. The easy way—which Rena called a lazy lattice—was to lay them all down in one direction first, then put the rest on top of them at right angles. But for a true lattice you had to intertwine the strips—under, then over, under, then over—as though you were weaving a basket. That was the only kind they ever made.

Thinking about it made Ginny long to be back in her grandfather's house on Madaket Road, in that narrow little kitchen, with the sound of the ocean coming through the sliding doors. Closing her eyes, she could picture the warm light filling the house, her mother perched on a stool smiling as Ginny laid ribbons of soft dough over the heaped berries.

She took a deep breath and tried to focus on the present. This wasn't doing any good, this endless wishing. She vowed to stop it.

"Come on," she told Daisy.

The woods and clearing around the Iron Age village were full of riches: huge, overgrown blackberry bushes; delicate purple dewberries growing low to the ground; even, here and there, a cluster of wild strawberries.

It was early in the season yet, but there would be a few ripe ones. They could always add a little honey to sweeten them up if they needed to.

Daisy was enchanted when Ginny showed her the tiny dewberries. With practiced hands Ginny scooped them up between slightly parted fingers, protecting their delicate skins. Daisy could not manage this, tending to pinch them in the middle as she plucked them from the stem. She would just sit there, amazed, gazing at the mashed berry between her fingers.

"Oops!" Ginny would say, "you're going to have to eat that one."

After a while Ginny's back began to ache from stooping. "Let's move on," she said.

They found a patch of wild strawberries, and Ginny added a few ripe ones to their minuscule pile of dewberries.

There were just about enough to make one little tart, she thought, discouraged. This would definitely not be dessert for fourteen.

Daisy was growing bored. She pulled out Lulu again. Oh, no, thought Ginny, not the bouncing doll!

"Want to go visit your secret hiding place?" she asked.

"In the woods?"

"Sure. I want to see that little house again."

"Okay," Daisy said.

They returned to the path and entered the shady world of the forest. It was a lot nicer in there on a sunny day. Quite peaceful, in fact, and pleasantly cool.

"So, when did you build the house?" Ginny asked, making conversation.

"When they were building the big one."

"The roundhouse? When you came out here on weekends to get everything ready last winter?"

Daisy nodded.

"Wasn't it cold?"

Daisy nodded again. "But we had on real clothes."

"Ah, yes," Ginny said dreamily, "real clothes . . ."

"They made a trap to catch pheasants, but Hugh said they shouldn't do it."

"Shouldn't catch the pheasants?"

"Uh-huh."

"Why—is it against the law?"

Daisy shrugged. "I don't know. He said because there weren't any pheasants back then."

"In the Iron Age?"

"Yes."

Ginny chuckled. This was probably the only five-year-old in the world who was in possession of that particular piece of information.

"So, do the boys still come out here?"

"No. Nat says it's a *baby* house."

"Well, too bad for him," Ginny said. "I think it's really cool."

They arrived at the copse of trees with the little structure carefully hidden behind it. That had been part of the plan, Ginny realized. That was why it was off the path and situated where it was. So it would be secret. For some reason Ginny found this terribly touching.

She looked around the small clearing. It was a charming place, with dappled patches of sunlight and—wonder of wonders—a great big blackberry bush on the far side. The fruit was still green, but later it would be fun to come out here and have a little snack whenever they wanted. The river was close by, for swimming. It was a perfect place to hang out on a summer day.

"Let's fix up the house!" Ginny said suddenly.

Daisy gazed up at her, curious.

"Make it really nice," Ginny explained. "You know, build a proper roof, cover the walls with mud."

"Daub," Daisy corrected.

"Aren't you the smart one?" Ginny said. "Same thing."

"No, daub's got stuff in it," she said.

"Like what?"

Daisy thought hard. "Straw," she said finally. "And other

104

stuff, maybe." Probably like the grog they worked into the clay, Ginny realized. It would hold the mud together when it dried.

"Will you help me?" Ginny asked.

Daisy nodded excitedly.

For the next hour they kept busy removing the debris from the collapsed roof and tidying up the clearing. As she worked, Ginny began building the new roof in her head, making a list of things she would need. Five or six straight poles for support. To get those, she'd probably have to cut down saplings, then chop off the branches. Then she'd need some smaller branches, green ones that she could bend into a ring beam. And something to tie it all together. When they got back to the compound, she would study the way the big roof was made and copy it on a small scale. She wondered whether she could just walk off with an ax. She'd probably have to ask her dad.

Ginny studied the structure of the walls. Not bad, she thought, considering that a couple of kids had built it. The whole thing leaned a bit, but she easily pushed it back into shape. When the walls were solid, it would stay put.

Daisy had gone off to the riverbank and was sitting there quietly, engrossed in something. Ginny let her be, following her old baby-sitting rule that you never interrupt a child who is happily playing by herself. But eventually she grew curious and just a little guilty. Daisy might have found a nice snake to play with or might be nibbling hemlock.

"Whatcha doing?"

Daisy looked up. She held a little mud figure in her hand. "It's Lulu's horsey," she said.

"That's nice," Ginny said. "Can I see it?"

Daisy handed it to her. It was rather sweet in a lumpy, nonrepresentational way. With its catlike head, flat back, enormous tail, and legs like an elephant, the one animal it didn't resemble in any way was a horse.

"This is really good," Ginny said.

"I want to cook it."

"Fire it, you mean?"

"Yeah."

"Daisy, it has to be clay to fire it in the kiln," Ginny explained gently.

"This is clay."

Ginny looked closer, smoothed it with her thumb. It did feel like clay, but it was gray, not red. "Where did you get this?" she asked.

"There." She pointed to the riverbank.

Ginny knelt and dug out a lump with a stick. She worked it around in her hands. It was clay, all right, and full of all kinds of junk: roots, pebbles, flints, dead plant material. You wouldn't have to wedge any grog into it at all, she thought. Ginny remembered what Mark had said that day: The clay was too pure; they weren't adding enough grog to it.

"Look, Daisy," she said, squatting down, "you can't fire your horsey right away, you know. First you have to let it dry."

"Oh," Daisy said, clearly disappointed.

"So why don't we keep it out here till it's dry? Then it'll be a surprise." Ginny handed the horse back to Daisy and sat down beside her. "I'll make something too."

She began to roll the clay out into slender little "snakes," as Mark had called them. Then, carefully, she began coiling the snakes up in the shape of a pot. She knew to make the sides curve up at the right angle for stability, having learned the hard way what happened if she didn't. When she had the shape right, she began to rub the coils into a smooth shape. She held it out at arm's length and turned it in her hands. It looked good. She added handles to the top and punched a design of shallow holes around the rim with a stick as finishing touches.

"I'm hungry," Daisy said finally.

"Oh, gosh! It's probably lunchtime." Ginny stood up, feeling stiff from sitting so long. "We'll come back after lunch and make a drying rack for our things. Just to keep them out of the rain. And we'll bring tools to start fixing up the house."

Daisy jumped up and down with delight.

Then they washed their hands, picked up the basket, and headed back.

"Don't forget Lulu," Ginny said, stopping suddenly.

Daisy gave Ginny a *silly me!* look, cute enough to get her hired for a cereal commercial, and scampered back to retrieve her doll.

Chapter 8

GINNY STOOD OUTSIDE the roundhouse in the dim light of early morning. Overhead a few stars still shimmered in the western sky. To the east, beyond the trees, the first bright sliver of sun peeked over the hills. Ginny trembled as a cool breeze brushed across her bare arms and ruffled her hair, like the comforting touch of some unseen, loving spirit. At that moment it seemed to her that nothing bad could possibly happen in such a perfect world.

The compound was strangely quiet. Besides Hugh and Ginny, only Faith and Millie were up, milking the goats, while in the roundhouse the placid sound of steady breathing mixed with droning snores. Ginny felt oddly special, as though she had been personally chosen to witness the birth of this new day.

She gathered a load of wood and shuffled back into the roundhouse. There she found Hugh bent over the hearth, feeding kindling to the coals. In the darkness the firelight gave his face a demonic glow.

Ginny inspected the breakfast porridge, all the while making mental plans for the day; there would be a lot to do. It had merely been luck that their turn in the cooking rotation had fallen on this particular day, the eve of Lugnasa. It was a big event, and the only festival Ginny would experience at the farm. Since most of the food would be prepared in advance, that meant Ginny would be making it. She couldn't wait to tell her mother that she had cooked a holiday dinner for sixteen without the benefit of any modern appliances. Rena would be impressed.

Back when Ginny first arrived, Mark had put forward his idea for rearranging the cooking teams to include her. Jonas had objected, apparently thinking of Ginny as a mere child, in the same category with Daisy and his two little boys. He had condescendingly asked her whether she knew anything at all about cooking. Ginny had been livid but kept her cool. "Trust me," she had said, "I can cook." Then she set out to prove it.

It wasn't going to be hard, Ginny knew. The standards she had to rise to were appallingly low. She had briefly wondered whether they were making everything bland and mushy on purpose, on the ground that Iron Age people would have been lousy cooks. Then Ginny reminded herself that they were English and that while the English were famous for many things—literature, for example, and empire building—food was not one of them.

On her very first attempt she had amazed one and all with her "garlic bread" (made by adding wild garlic to the dough before baking) and a richly flavored stew to which she had added sorrel, thyme, wild onion, fresh beans, and dried chanterelle mushrooms. Even Jonas was generous in his praise. She felt very smug that night.

Now, on this special occasion, she hoped to outdo herself. She had been planning the menu for days and couldn't wait to get started. It wasn't just that she wanted everyone to have a good time, though of course she did. It was something more. She knew she would be leaving soon, and it had begun to trouble her that their lives would go on without her, day after day, until before long it would be as if she had never even been there. Ginny thought that if she gave them this special day, this wonderful feast, then they would remember her.

Faith came in with the milk. Some of it would go into the porridge with a bit left over for drinking, though the prejudice against warm milk was strong. The remainder would be set aside in the storehouse to sour. Once the milk had curdled, it was hung up in a linen bag for the whey to drip out. The result was the soft, creamy cheese they ate every day.

The people were beginning to wake now, and one by one they wandered past the hearth on their way to the lavatory. Then they returned to sit by the fire and eat their bowls of porridge with milk and honey. Nobody was very chatty at breakfast.

Ginny had already eaten, so she got started at the quern. By now she was a seasoned pro. With one hand, she scooped up some grain from the basket nearby and dribbled it into the central hole in the top stone. With the other, she kept it spinning. Soft puffs of white flour drifted out around the lower edge and collected on the goatskin below.

She had grown to like the steady grinding of stone against stone. It was monotonous and calming. Maybe, Ginny thought, the Sharper Image should add it to its sleep-sound machines: "quern sounds." It could go between "waterfall" and "desert sunrise."

As she worked, Ginny's mind returned to the same thought that had hovered in there for days—what news Maurice might bring when he came tomorrow. A letter, surely, but maybe more. It was even remotely possible that he might say that her mother had called and Ginny was going home. She might even drive back with him that very day.

She told herself not to get her hopes up. After all, there were three whole weeks until school started. Still, she found herself trying to imagine how it would all play out. They would have to go by the university to retrieve her suitcase, and surely there would be someplace where she could shower and wash her hair and change clothes before going to the airport. That is, if there was a flight that night. She had a vague memory that there were only morning flights to Houston, in which case she'd have to spend the night somewhere. Please, God, not with Maurice!

Corey was the last one up, as usual. He seemed to need an awful lot of sleep. Faith practically had to drag him out of bed most mornings, but since his return from the hospital she had pretty much let him alone.

By the time he awoke, all the others had finished eating and gone outside. Hugh was in the storeroom, so Ginny was alone. There was something excitingly intimate about seeing Corey shuffle sleepily out of his room, eyes half-open, hair hanging in his face.

"Good morning," Ginny said with a perkiness she hoped was annoying.

He smiled dreamily and grunted.

"I saved you some porridge," she said.

Ginny noticed with pleasure that his face was no longer alarming. The horrible blisters now looked like nothing worse than a case of teenage acne. In a few weeks his complexion would be beautiful again.

"I'd like some egg, sausage, and tomato with that," he said, taking the porridge and sitting cross-legged on a sheepskin to eat it.

Ginny gave an exaggerated shudder of disgust. "Ugh—English breakfast!"

Corey laughed. "Looking forward to tomorrow?"

"Yes, but I'm not sure what to expect. You had one of these festivals before. What was it like?"

"Yeah. Beltain, it was called. May Day. But it was different. We had a Maypole and a May Queen and all that."

"May Queen? Who was it?"

"Three guesses, but you'll only need one."

"Liz?"

"Of course."

Ginny sighed. It must be really something to be so beautiful that people automatically made you the queen of things. It was not something she'd ever have to worry about. In the looks department she was intensely, extremely, profoundly average.

"So what all goes on tomorrow?" she asked.

"What all?" he said, imitating her Texas accent. "Well, there's supposed to be wrestling and a tug-of-war and maybe some races. Also, putting the rock," he said, pantomiming the action of flinging an imaginary rock from shoulder level. "I gather we can expect some hilarity, what with the mead they've been brewing so carefully."

"Mead?"

"It's like wine, only made from honey," he said.

Great—a drunken sporting event, Ginny thought. She hoped everybody wouldn't get dopey. She hoped they wouldn't spoil her perfect day.

Corey yawned and stretched, an amused look on his face.

"What?" asked Ginny.

"Oh, nothing," he said in that lilting way. "Just thinking about something."

"Well, it's obviously pretty funny." Ginny prompted him.

"Yeah, I guess. It's just this pub we passed on the way back from the hospital. I kept begging Maurice to stop and let us go in, and he just kept driving."

"Sounds like Maurice."

"So Faith and me, we got to ragging him about it. "'Oh, just some chips!'" we'd say. "'Just a bit of cheese!'" "'Oh, I've got such a dreadful thirst!'" We were just having a bit of fun with him, you know, but all of a sudden he slams on the brakes, turns around, and goes back to that pub!"

"You had a whole meal there?"

"Yes, we did. And Maurice did too!" Corey laughed, slapping his thighs. "I think we made him hungry."

"So, what was it like, being back in the real world after all this time out here?"

"Well, I wouldn't call a hospital the real world."

"You know what I mean."

"Yeah," he said, and thought a bit. "Well, this'll sound odd, but it was bright—bright colors, I mean. And noisy."

"But you got to sleep in a real bed and take a shower."

"Yeah, that was good. And the pub lunch was good too."

"Did you get to see your girlfriend?" Ginny asked. She had been searching for a way to introduce this topic ever since he got back. She was dying to know whether she had visited him in the hospital or she had decided that a year was too long to wait for a guy—even one as cute as Corey.

"Mia? No, I didn't get to see her at all. We weren't in London, you know, just the local place. I did talk to her on the phone, though." Then, with a wicked grin: "I told her about you."

"Yeah?" Ginny said, surprised.

"Yeah."

"So, what did you say?"

"I said you had beautiful eyes." Then he laughed.

Ginny didn't know whether he was giving her a compliment or making fun of her. She blushed fiercely and looked down at her hands.

"You do, you know," he said reassuringly. "Plus I just thought I'd make her a little jealous."

"So, did it work?"

"Nah. Nothing fazes Mia." Corey finished eating and rinsed out his bowl. Then, brushing his dark hair back out of his eyes, he gave her a friendly smile and left.

Sometime after lunch Ginny told Hugh she would be gone for a while. She had a surprise treat in mind and needed to go find the raw materials for it. She was a little disappointed that he didn't beg to know what it was; she would have told him, since he'd find out anyway when she made them. But he just said okay and went about his business.

"He has no sense of occasion": Rena had said that once about Hugh when Ginny's birthday present had arrived three days late. He hadn't made the extra effort to make sure it arrived on time, nor had he bothered to gift-wrap it. Just plain brown mailing paper. At least there had been a card, though it didn't appear that he had spent much time picking it out. It was one of those sappy ones with flowers on it. "For a Dear Daughter," it had said.

Ginny picked up a basket and left the roundhouse. She had scarcely left the compound when Daisy spotted her and darted out in her direction.

"Not today, Daisy," Ginny called loud enough for Liz to hear. "I'm the cook today."

"Are you going to . . . you know?" Daisy asked in a stage whisper.

"I'm going to pick berries."

"I want to come! Please!"

Ginny didn't mind, really, except that she was afraid that when she got back, she wouldn't be able to get rid of her.

"I'll help!" Daisy offered sweetly. Ginny weakened. The expression on Daisy's face was so earnest, the prayerful gesture of her tiny hands so charming Ginny couldn't resist. As she looked at that eager face, it struck her that Daisy had changed. The desperation was gone; she wasn't on edge all the time. Maybe she was finally settling in.

"We're just going to pick berries," Ginny said as Daisy caught up with her. "I am going to our special place, but only because there's that blackberry bush there. Okay? There's no time to work on the house because I have to cook today, and tomorrow is a big party, you know."

"I know!" Daisy chirped, skipping alongside her.

There were many more ripe berries now, and the girls quickly filled the basket with strawberries and blackberries. Ginny even devised an Iron Age blackberry hook from a gnarled branch. She pulled the tall branches down, and Daisy captured the berries. "Watch out for thorns," she warned.

They finished up with the big bush at their special place. Ginny couldn't resist stopping there for a moment, to admire the stunning transformation they had achieved in just a week.

She hadn't even known what she was doing at first, since she hadn't been there when the compound was built. But then she realized that all she had to do was ask her dad, anything at all. He was delighted to answer her questions, assuming that she had suddenly developed a burning interest in Iron Age building techniques—which, in fact, she had.

"So, how do you make daub?" she had asked, to which Hugh responded with a recipe: two parts clay to one part dirt. To that you added straw and some binding material, such as wool or pig's bristle. This was mixed with enough water to get the right consistency, then slapped into the wattle framework from both sides.

Then there was the problem of tools. She asked permission to borrow some, explaining that she and Daisy were making a little playhouse in the woods. This was something of an understatement, but it was the truth. Hugh was glad to lend them, so long as they weren't needed on the farm that day. He just made her promise to use them safely, especially with Daisy around.

Making the daub and applying it to the walls had been a big, messy job that took two whole days. First Ginny had to dig up all that dirt and clay. Then she had to mix it with straw and shredded bits of wool. Her back and arms were sore for days afterward. But actually applying it to the framework had been fun. They both stripped to their underwear, Daisy on the inside of the building, Ginny on the outside, each with a bucket of daub. Then they had a mud fight.

"Don't get me in the face," Ginny warned, throwing a big muddy glob at the wall. It was amazing how much of it stuck where it belonged, though a certain amount went right through and landed on Daisy. She just scooped it up and added it to her side. Little by little the wicker structure was filled solid, inside and out.

Afterward they could have been mistaken for the daughters of Bigfoot or perhaps the Monsters from the Slime.

"Do you know how to swim?" Ginny asked. Daisy said she didn't.

The riverbank was steep there. You couldn't just wade in.

"Let me get in the water first and get washed off; then I'll carry you in and give you a lesson."

They had stayed in the water for quite a while. It felt so good to be clean again, and the water was wonderfully cool and clear. Ginny even showed Daisy the dead man's float, and taught her how to dog-paddle. "It's not pretty," Ginny said, "but it will get you to the edge of the river if you ever fall in."

As the walls had dried, they were cracked in places, so Ginny made up a small batch of daub and repaired them. They were now a solid gray-white, more or less smooth, and without visible cracks.

The roof beams were up too, and she had almost finished tying on the horizontal rings of hazel branches that would make the roof stronger and act as a support for the thatch. It was tempting to stay and work on it for an hour or so.

Ginny wasn't sure how long it was going to take her to finish the roof, but the thatching would go slowly, she knew that much. She had already decided on a simplified version of a true thatched roof, because she had neither the skill nor the time to make the real thing. But she could bundle up dried grass and lay it over the roof well enough to keep the rain out—not for fifty years maybe, but for a while at least. And that way she could get it all finished before she left. Ginny really wanted to do that.

"You know what, Daisy?" she said. "I think I'd like to give our place a name."

"Okay," Daisy said.

"You don't mind? I mean, it was your place first."

Daisy shrugged. "It's okay," she said again.

"Well, I was just thinking, there's a really pretty psalm— do you know what a psalm is?"

"No."

"Like in church? In the Bible?"

"Yeah."

"Well, this psalm is really nice, it's like a poem, you know? And it's sort of peaceful, like this place. Happy. And it has a line about 'still waters' in it that seems perfect. Don't you think that would be a good name, with the river and all? Still Waters?"

"Yeah," Daisy said.

"Good."

Ginny suddenly had a picture of herself, a grown woman, coming back here someday—with her husband maybe. For some reason she was in black and white and dressed in one of those long, slim skirts women wore in the thirties. She had short curls and wore a hat. She was in a movie. She said to her husband, who was very handsome and had slicked-back hair, "It's around here somewhere."

They'd wander around in the woods; that would be hard to do in high heels, but suddenly she would find it. "Here it is," she'd say in a thirties movie fake English accent.

They both would stand and stare in wonder at this charming little house in the woods, which would still be in perfect condition. Maybe ivy or roses or something would have grown up over the wall. Then Ginny would sit down delicately on a log and say something wistful to her handsome husband. What would she say? Maybe just "I was happy here." Then the music would rise, and the camera would pull back slowly until the two people and the little house were lost in the trees.

Daisy had wandered over to the drying rack. Five pots, Lulu's horse, a rather squashed-looking angel, a second horse for Lulu, and a little dog sat there now. She had taken them down and arranged them in two facing groups. Maybe they were going to have a war.

"Not now, Daisy," Ginny said. "Time to go."

Daisy dutifully put the combatants back on the rack.

"Say bye to Still Waters," Ginny said.

"Bye, Still Waters," Daisy said sweetly.

Then Ginny picked up the basket of berries and herded Daisy back to the compound. "Now listen," Ginny said firmly when they arrived. "I'm making a big surprise for tomorrow, and it won't be any fun if you see it now. So you need to go back to your mom, okay?"

Daisy said okay, her eyes wide with the anticipation of good things to come. She skipped off to where Liz was weaving a basket, and Ginny went inside the roundhouse.

Sitting near the hearth, she began preparing a sweet dough, adding butter to make it flaky. When she was finished kneading it, she set it near the fire to rest. There was a popular theory among the villagers that a certain amount of yeast was naturally present in the wheat, so it might actually rise a little if you set it in a warm place. While the dough was doing its thing, Ginny added honey to the berries, then delicately stirred in flour to thicken the juices. She rolled out the dough on a large, flat board and cut it into four-inch squares. In the center of each she put a dollop of blackberry filling, then folded the squares into triangles, pinching the edges to seal them. With a knife she carefully cut tiny parallel slits on top of each tart for the steam to escape. Probably some blackberry syrup would escape too, but that would be all right. She couldn't wait to see everyone's expression when she produced them next day.

Jonas was there, grinding away at the quern. It had been going all day, with each of the villagers taking a turn, since they would need enough flour for that day's baking, plus lots more for Lugnasa.

"That looks rather exotic," Jonas said.

"I'd like this to be a surprise," Ginny said.

"My lips are sealed," he promised.

Hugh came in with a basket full of freshly picked peas. He sat down on a sheepskin, grabbed another basket and a big bowl, and began shelling them—husks in the basket, peas in the bowl. After a while he looked up at Ginny. "What's that?" he asked.

"It's a surprise," Ginny and Jonas said together.

"They can torture me. I won't tell," said Hugh. "Blackberries?"

"Mixed with strawberries."

"Gracious!" he said, like she had just invented the cotton gin. Hugh sat there with a thoughtful expression on his face, popping open the fat green pods and scooping out the tender peas. Then he looked up and watched Ginny for a while.

"You know," he said finally, "I had no idea you were so competent."

"Competent? Because I can make tarts?"

"I mean . . ." He paused to gather his thoughts. "You're so adaptable and have so many skills. Frankly, when Rena asked if you could come out here, I was worried. I didn't think you could make it."

"I didn't think I could either at first," Ginny said.

"But it's more than that, you know? You're inventive. You don't just go along; you reach for more."

Ginny sat perfectly still.

"I didn't express it very well," Hugh said.

"No, no—it was nice," Ginny said. "Thanks."

It had to be the strangest compliment she had ever received. Usually people complimented things like the clothes you wore, or your hair or eyes. Or they said you were smart or polite. Her dad had said she was strong. Ginny liked that.

When the last of the tarts was ready to go, Ginny slipped them onto the stone shelf at the back of the oven. Hugh raked out most of the coals from the front and closed the oven door. Or, to be more precise, he leaned a flat stone against the opening and stopped up any gaps with chunks of turf, or turves as he called them. They were the raggedy country cousins of those squares of sod used at home to start an instant lawn in a new yard. It seemed like a strange thing to use in a kitchen, but Hugh said the soil was a good heat insulator, the grass and roots held it all together, and it was flexible, so you could fit it into odd angles.

The complicated nature of this makeshift door plus the fact that the oven worked on accumulated heat from the dying coals made baking tricky. It wasn't only that you never knew how hot the oven was. You couldn't peek in all that often to see what was going on in there either.

Ginny set her mental oven timer, then moved on to make that evening's stew. The salted meat that had been soaking was ready by now, so she drained it and put it in the pot. It always bothered her to handle meat there, because she had no soap to wash her hands with. Her mother was fanatical about cleanliness in the kitchen, especially with meat and chicken. Rena scrubbed everything—cutting board, knife, hands—with hot water and lots of detergent. Ginny had to admit, though, that so far no one had gotten sick from the food.

She cut large horse mushrooms into bite-size chunks and added them to the meat. She had picked some little fairy ring mushrooms, too, but their delicate flavor would be lost in the hearty stew. She decided to put them in with the peas instead, along with wild onions and butter and maybe even some mint.

Ginny got up and removed one of the turves from the opening. A blast of hot air hit her face as she peered inside the oven. The pastry wasn't brown yet.

"You know what they say about a watched pot," said Jonas.

"Yeah, it never boils over," said Ginny.

"Also, remember that you lose heat every time you do that."

Ginny sighed. Jonas had unfortunate know-it-all tendencies, magnified in her presence by the fact that in the real world he was a science teacher. He could never resist being the person who told you things. Ginny had to admit that she had actually learned quite a lot from him and his little lectures, but she always hated the sense of inequality it gave them. Out here, with the exception of Daisy and the wild boys, they all were equals. When Jonas slipped into his teacher mode, she shifted back to being a kid.

Ginny scooped a big handful of dried beans out of the storage basket and put them in the stew, then cut up big chunks of wild onion and garlic. She would have to go out in search of thyme or wild chervil for seasoning once the tarts were done.

When she could stand it no longer, Ginny moved the stone door from the oven and peered in again, then let out a little gasp of delight. Her tarts were golden brown, runnels of purple juice oozing out here and there. Carefully she removed them from the oven. Hugh and Jonas both came over to look.

"Oh, they're beautiful!" Hugh said, leaning over to admire them with his hands clasped behind his back. He looked like a preschooler whose teacher had told him *Don't touch!*

"Well, my dear," said Jonas grandly, "now you know how Leonardo felt when he painted the *Mona Lisa!*"

At that moment Ginny felt unaccountably happy. It was such a small thing, really, she told herself—to make something pretty that would taste good, to set out to do something and have it turn out well. But then most of the happy moments she had ever known were over little things. It wasn't how you'd think it'd be, but that's the way it was.

Ginny's foraging trip took a little longer than she had planned. There was really so much to gather, and thanks to Karen, she could now recognize a lot of the edible plants that grew wild in the forest and meadow. She knew where to find special things, like mint and thyme, pignuts and watercress. Others were practically everywhere you looked, such as ransoms, a kind of wild garlic. When her basket was full, she gathered a bouquet of fragrant meadowsweet, flowers for the table.

On her way back Ginny ran into Tom and Ian at the edge of the clearing. They were busy tying a rope to the hind legs of a Shetland ram. Ginny stood there, her arms full of flowers, curious to know what they were doing. It was the wrong season for shearing.

The ram stood there stupidly, unmindful of the rope on its hind legs or the unrelenting barking of Flora, who watched with trembling excitement from a distance of about four feet. Tom took the loose end of the rope and threw it over a stout limb of the overhanging tree. Then he squatted down beside the ram and wrapped his big arms around its neck, muttering sweet endearments to it in the same gentle tones he used when he talked to Daisy.

"Okay," said Tom in a level voice. "Please get the ram and not me."

Ian leaned over and picked up a large fencing mallet, which was lying in the grass. "Bucket ready?" he asked.

Tom slid a large bucket into place near the ram's head.

All at once Ginny knew what was about to happen, but she couldn't seem to move her legs. She stood there like she was playing statues until suddenly, with barely enough time for her to shut her eyes, there was a sharp thud, the crack of bone, the whiz of the rope sliding over the limb, being pulled taut. When she dared look, she saw the ram now hanging head down, its slit throat disgorging blood into the bucket.

Flora dashed in excitedly to lick the blood as it fell. Ian kicked her away. Ginny thought she was going to throw up. She turned her back on the scene and walked unsteadily back toward the compound. Just once she turned to look back and wished she hadn't. Ian had slit the belly of the ram open, and the intestines slid out smoothly into the bucket. She leaned over the grassy verge of the path and vomited. Her whole body felt as if it had been delivered an electric shock. Shaking and weak, she returned to the village. As she stumbled through the gate, she saw Corey watching her.

"It's hard, the first time you see it," he said.

Ginny nodded slowly, wiping away tears.

"That's tomorrow's roast, you know."

Ginny felt the sour taste of bile in her mouth. She leaned over and spit it into the ditch.

"You'll get over it, though," he said gently.

"It's horrible."

"It's a fact of life. It's nothing new."

"It's new to me."

"Yeah, I understand. But you know, if you're going to eat meat at all—well, our animals here, their lives aren't bad," Corey said. "Rather cushy, in fact. Not like on big commercial farms. I don't think that little ram suffered a minute in his life, right to the very end."

Ginny was thinking that maybe she should become a vegetarian. "So, how come you're always around to cheer me up at the worst times?" she said, her voice hoarse and throaty.

"Oh, didn't you know?" said Corey, taking the basket and escorting her back to the roundhouse. "I'm your guardian angel."

Chapter 9

WHEN GINNY WOKE up on the morning of Lugnasa, she had a powerful sense that the day would be memorable and life-changing. She thought this must be the way she would feel on her wedding day. Something she had chosen, planned, and looked forward to for a long time had suddenly arrived. And now she wasn't sure how she felt about it.

The nearness of change thrilled and terrified her. Soon she would be back with her mom in Houston, living her real life, seeing her friends, sleeping in her own bed. The long exile would be over. But at the same time, she felt a strange regret at the very thought of leaving this odd life and these people she had come to know so well. She understood that they would not drop out of her consciousness as she drove away. They would leave a hole in her soul.

The group was sitting outside the roundhouse, waiting for Maurice and trying to get things organized. Lazy and luxurious, they sprawled about like sunbathers, arguing playfully. The subject of discussion was wrestling, which they felt they had to include in the day's activities for the sake of historical accuracy. All the ancient sources mentioned it as one of the highlights of every Celtic festival.

The problem was, nobody really wanted to do it, not even Ian and Tom, the only ones who knew how.

Jonas suggested that a demonstration match between the two might meet the technical requirements, to which Ian howled in protest. "Why not just kill me now and get it over with?" he said.

The picture of a David and Goliath match struck everyone as pretty funny, but they all agreed it wasn't fair. That left them back at square one. Finally it was Sam who solved the problem. "What about arm wrestling?" he said. The idea was greeted with spontaneous cheering and even some random animal noises. It occurred to Ginny that if the group was already this merry at breakfast time, things could get pretty wild when the mead started flowing.

The wrestling dealt with, they moved on to working out the teams for the tug-of-war and the rules for putting the rock. They had gotten so noisy that none of them noticed that Maurice and Roger had arrived until they strolled through the gate, armed to the teeth with equipment.

"Started drinking already?" Maurice asked dryly.

This comment was met with boos and hisses. Flora joined in with urgent barks and ran over to scamper around at their feet and generally get in the way.

Maurice, the bringer of mail! Ginny was suddenly as nervous as a racehorse. She leaped to her feet and ran to him. "Is there a letter for me?" she asked breathlessly.

"Hold on," Maurice said, laying his equipment down and opening up his briefcase. He went through the mail so slowly and deliberately that Ginny half suspected he was stringing her along out of spite. He found letters for Jonas and Liz, who were standing nearby, then finally handed one to Ginny.

She would have preferred to go off and find some remote and private spot to read it, as she had before, but now she was too impatient. Over behind the henhouse would have to do. She leaned against the fence and tore the envelope open.

The first thing she noticed was her mother's handwriting. It looked messy, as though she had written the letter on horseback or in the car. The script got larger, then smaller, almost trailing off in places. Ginny found this alarming.

> *Dear Ginny,*
>
> *Thank you for your sweet letter. I miss you too, very much. But it comforts me to know that you are there having an adventure with your father and that the two of you are getting to know each other. He wrote to say that you are quite the clever girl, but then you always were.*
>
> *I'm afraid I don't have much interesting news to write about. My life seems to revolve around going back and forth to the hospital these days. But please don't you fret, sweetheart. I have a very good doctor here and have*

begun a course of treatment. It's very aggressive—that's the word the doctor used, and it's the right word too. I'm going to be very sick for a while, but chances are good I'll be back to my old self after it's all over. How long that will take, I don't exactly know yet. I beg you to bear with me patiently if you can.

I asked Maud to keep Sophie for a while, but you will be happy to know that her puppies arrived just fine. Maud is getting the pictures developed now, so I'll send them along with the next letter. She says the puppies are adorable.

Hang in there, darling, and I will do the same.

I love you!!!
Mom

P.S. There are five puppies!

That was it?

Ginny felt her face flush, her head buzz. And it shocked her to realize suddenly that what she was feeling right then was not grief or sorrow—it was wild, screaming anger. She wanted to kick something. She wanted to shriek. It took all her willpower and several minutes for her to gather her composure. Then she went to look for her dad.

She found him leaning against the door to the roundhouse, several pages of cream-colored stationery in his hand. "That's from my mom, isn't it?" Ginny demanded.

He looked up slowly, his eyes bright. "Yes, it is," he said.

"Why didn't you tell me before that she was writing to you?"

He shrugged. "Why should it surprise you?"

"Well, you haven't written to each other for the last *eight years!*"

"Actually, Ginny, that's not true—though we don't write very often, I'll grant you that, and it's always about you."

"Will you tell me what she said?"

"When I finish reading it." Ginny stood there waiting impatiently, shifting from one foot to the other. His letter was several pages long, she noticed. Why would Rena have so much more to say to him than she did to her? The only explanation Ginny could think of was that Rena was hiding something.

Hugh folded the letter and put it back in the envelope. He cleared his throat. "It's mostly about her medical condition," he began. "She thought it would be better if I explained it to you. There's a lot of technical stuff that, I'm afraid, is a bit beyond me. But the crucial part is that when they did the operation, they found that a lot of the lymph nodes were involved."

"I already know that," Ginny said. Then she thought for a minute. "What does that mean exactly?"

"Well," he said, and Ginny sensed reluctance in his voice, "I gather it means the cancer has spread."

Real grief came over her then, beginning with an ache around the heart, then rising into her throat and contorting her face into a grimace of despair. She stood there with her arms hanging down and her anguished face upraised for a few seconds, until Hugh reached out and hugged her.

When she had cried herself out, he held her out at arm's length and studied her gravely. "I know it's scary for you to hear these things, Ginny, but I don't want you to get carried away. This is just a bump in the road, that's all. Your mother is at one of the top cancer centers in the world, and she's undergoing a very sophisticated treatment, a bone marrow transplant. It could cure her completely, she says."

Ginny grew suddenly excited. "A bone marrow transplant? Doesn't she need a donor for that? Shouldn't I be tested? I'm her closest relative." She had seen it in a movie.

"No," Hugh said, "it's not that kind. They take her own cells and freeze them and then give them back to her later, after she's had all the chemotherapy."

"Oh," Ginny said, disappointed. "Did she say anything about me coming home?" Ginny already knew the answer.

"Not for a while," he said.

"Were those her actual words, or are you just assuming that?"

"Ginny—try to have some patience. I know it's hard, and I know you feel confused, but sometimes you just have to stop fretting and let things play out."

Wait, trust, have patience. Go away and stop asking questions: That's what everybody was really saying.

They went inside the roundhouse and sat side by side, gazing at the cook fire, where the ram roasted slowly on the spit. Bits of juice dripped onto the coals occasionally, hissing softly. Already it had the smell of cooking meat.

Outside, the others had evidently finished reading their mail. They were beginning to grow noisy again.

"I can't go out there and play games," Ginny said flatly.

Hugh stroked his beard distractedly for a while. "Ginny, it won't help your mother get better for you to mope around and refuse to have fun."

"I don't care. I just don't feel like it."

"Well, I think it's a mistake," Hugh said. "There's nothing that drives sorrow out like laughter."

"Nobody laughs when they're sad!" Ginny said, disgusted.

"People do, actually. And it helps a lot. May I tell you a story?"

Ginny shrugged.

"I had an aunt, my father's older sister, Abigail. She was a wonderful lady, quite the world traveler and very artistic. She was always running off to India or Argentina and coming home with boatloads of odd stuff—sculptures, masks, embroideries. She was quite modern and worldly too, for an elderly spinster lady. Had a wicked wit, embarrassed my father no end."

"She sounds like my mom," Ginny said.

"Yes, she was rather like Rena in many ways," he said. He paused as if considering that. "Hunh!" he muttered.

"What?"

He shook his head. "Never mind," he said. "Anyway, she was a great storyteller and limerick writer and had a natural way with children. I remember there was this great mystery about her name. It was Abigail B. Dorris, and she would never tell anyone what the *B* stood for. She said it was just too awful. It became a sort of guessing game among the nieces and nephews. We finally decided it had to be Beulah, since that was a family name. But she never admitted to it."

"Why didn't you just ask your dad?"

Hugh laughed again. "I did. He hadn't the slightest idea."

"His own sister?"

"Exactly. You never knew your grandfather, or you wouldn't be so surprised. It's a shame that she was the one who never married and had a family. Rather ironic too, because she was the only adult in our lives who had any time for us at all, or that's how it seemed to me anyway."

He folded his arms on his knees and rested his chin there. "When Abigail died," he went on, "the mourners completely filled the church; quite a few had to stand. I rather think it amazed my father to see how many friends she had. Anyhow, the reception after the funeral was held at our house, and it just went on and on. Finally, most of the people went home, all but a few of her dearest friends. So we moved into the drawing room and got comfortable and started telling Abigail stories. Everybody remembered something funny or outrageous she had done, and before long we were all laughing like mad. Flopping on the floor laughing, literally! We kept it up for hours. I've never forgotten that night. It was like the last nice thing she gave us, all those wonderful memories. I only wished she could have been there to enjoy it."

They sat silently for a while. Then Hugh said, "It's the

only time I ever remember hearing my father laugh."

The ruckus outside indicated that the games had begun.

"It isn't the same!" Ginny blurted out suddenly. "You're talking like my mother is dead."

Hugh looked nonplussed. "That wasn't my intention at all!" he said. "Far from it! Your mother is working very hard to get well. All I meant was that sometimes it's all right to laugh, even when you feel sad. It's not disrespectful."

They heard their names being called outside.

"Come on, Ginny," Hugh said, pulling her to her feet. "I can tell you for a fact that your mother would want us to enjoy this beautiful day. You know she would. And if she were here right now, she'd be enjoying it too."

After Ginny had washed her face and taken a few deep breaths, she agreed to go outside. Everyone was sitting on the circle of logs, watching the men's arm wrestling tournament. Ian and Jonas sat facing each other with their elbows on a stump and their hands locked. They were showing off, entertaining the audience with fierce grunts and moans. The rest were cheering and laughing.

Ginny felt like the ghost at the feast. She tried on a wan smile, hoping to blend in and avoid being asked any questions. She didn't think she could handle that.

"It's okay, Ian," Millie was yelling. "He's a big'n, but he's a softy!"

"Who's a softy?" Jonas called back indignantly. While his attention was distracted, Ian gave a mighty push and Jonas's forearm went down. Everyone cheered.

Ginny thought it was really nice the way adults could sometimes put aside their dignity and play games like children. She found it comforting, somehow, and as the various rounds of the tournament progressed, her sadness began to fade away.

By midmorning it was already hot. The men's rock putting dragged on, since everyone got three tries and each throw was followed by lots of marking and measuring. It was not the sort of thing you could sit and watch full-time. The women sat waiting their turn and weaving flower crowns.

Ginny hadn't made one in years, probably not since third grade, when she and her friend Cecilia had ducked out of the games during recess to sit at the edge of the field and make dandelion crowns. Recess was supposed to be free time for the kids to do whatever they wanted, but Ginny's teacher didn't really support this idea. She thought recess was all about exercise. The flower crown thing had annoyed her, and she made the girls take them off before returning to the classroom.

Well, she's not here now, Ginny thought as she raked her hair with her fingers and arranged the crown carefully on her head. Wearing it made her feel carefree and playful, like a little kid in a simple world where nothing was ever complicated or confusing or sad. That was not the world Ginny lived in, but it was a nice place to visit every once in a while.

The day slipped by easily, the way it does at the beach. It even felt like that: the sun, the breeze, the sound of people playing games, the sense that your brain was getting baked but you didn't really care. All that was missing was the roar of the surf.

When the last rock had been put and lunch had been enjoyed, everyone pretty much gave up any pretense of organized activity. While Maurice did some interviews and Bunny and Jonas cleaned up the dishes, Ginny and the others returned to the meadow to nap in the sun.

"Want some writing paper?" Ginny opened her eyes to see Roger peering down at her.

She reached up to take the materials, and he strolled away. She sat for a moment, watching, as he went from one reclining person to another, handing out paper and pens, like someone distributing leaflets in the park.

She rubbed her eyes and tried to focus. What should she write? Part of her wanted badly to say a lot of serious things: Please, Mom, be straight with me. I want to hear directly from you, not through Dad. And I want to know just exactly how sick you are, and when I can come home. Please don't say "soon" or "I'll let you know." Please trust me enough to give me the truth.

It scared her to think of being that blunt. Was it because she didn't really want to hear the answers?

Maybe, instead, she should write something upbeat and entertaining, full of stories about life in the Iron Age. That would be a lot easier.

In the end she wrote both kinds of letter. She started out with life on the farm, introducing the cast of characters. On paper they all became slightly exaggerated versions of themselves—but vivid. Her mother would be able to see them with her mind's eye. Ginny invented so many witty and telling descriptions that she grew quite proud of her writing and hoped her mother would save the letter. Parts of it would make a great English paper. She could even call it "What I Did on My Summer Vacation."

She told about the episode of the swarming bees and how Corey went to the hospital. She said the pots kept breaking and she missed the plain old aluminum ones at home. She listed some of the wild foods she had learned to recognize. She described bathing in a barrel and washing her hair with clay. She told Rena who the Celts were and what Lugnasa was. Then she gave every detail of the special meal she had made for tonight, especially the blackberry tarts. She even drew a little picture of one.

There was only a half page left, but she wanted to tell her mother about Still Waters and the little roundhouse they were making out there, and especially about the mud fight. She began writing smaller to fit it all in. She told Rena it was a secret, and she wasn't to mention it to Hugh. That reminded her that the one thing her mom most cared about was how she was getting on with her dad, so she put that in too. "He doesn't quite know how to do the father thing," she wrote, "but I'm teaching him how."

Finally, with about two inches of paper left, she made her plea. She tried very hard to keep the anger out, but she wanted to be clear. Reading it over afterward, Ginny felt she had managed on both counts. It was not a request that could be ignored. "School starts in three weeks," she said.

"Please tell me on what day, between now and then, I will be flying home."

The tug-of-war had a last-game-of-the-day feel about it. They were all too mellow by then to get all that excited about it, and if the event hadn't already been planned, they might have skipped it altogether. The results were predictable: Half their number came back soaked from a dunking in the sheep pond, and all of them were tired. Ginny was glad she belonged to the dry half. The afternoon sun was low in the sky, and it was starting to cool off.

By the time the feast was served, a mood of relaxation and goodwill had settled over the group. Bunny and Jonas were the cooks for the day, but besides keeping the roast turning on the spit and warming things up, they had done very little. Ginny had made most of the food the day before.

They constructed a low serving table using logs and boards—Ginny called it the buffet—and right in the middle she put the bowl of meadowsweet. It looked so lovely that Bunny went out and got more flowers and greens to tuck in around the bowls and baskets.

The food was abundant: cream of mushroom soup, roast mutton, peas with mint and mushrooms, garlic herb bread and butter, braised hogweed, a salad of dandelion greens and watercress, garlic cheese spread, wild apples, honey, and lots of the promised mead.

There were supposed to have been eggs too. They had saved up seven of them, which Bunny had planned to hard-boil. That had seemed too ordinary to Ginny. Besides, how could you serve sixteen people with seven eggs? "Why don't I make an omelet?" she had suggested. "But I'll have to do it at the last minute so it won't be all cold and yucky."

Ginny had mixed the eggs with salt, thyme, and the tender shoots of the hop plant. That would add a rich flavor and a nice crunchiness. While Bunny and Jonas were setting out the dishes, Ginny melted some butter, whipped up the eggs, and poured the mixture in. Instantly the pot shattered, and a week's worth of eggs oozed into the fire. It made Ginny sick just to think about it. When you planned things carefully and really thought them through, it seemed to her that they ought to work out.

Corey came over and sat beside her, his bowl heaped with food. He was still damp from the sheep pond, and his clothes gave off a musty smell.

All around her, people were tucking into the feast with enthusiasm, tearing off bits of meat with their hands, slurping soup, scooping up peas with their fingers. With Corey sitting right next to her, Ginny grew suddenly self-conscious.

What would the Iron Age Emily Post recommend? Probably picking up one pea at a time between thumb and forefinger. That way in about a month she would be finished with her meal. She tried using her bread as a makeshift utensil and found that she could get small portions into her mouth pretty efficiently without dipping more than two or three fingers in the food.

She definitely should have mentioned that in her letter,

Ginny thought, with lots of gory details. Hurry, Mom, bring me home before my table manners vanish for good!

Corey watched her for a while, a teasing grin on his face. Ginny wondered what he thought was so funny.

"So, did yesterday push you over the edge?" Corey asked.

"What are you talking about?"

"You didn't take any meat."

Ginny sighed. "No," she said.

"Did you know that vegetables scream when you pull them out of the ground?" he said teasingly.

"Oh, get out of here," she said, irritated.

"So, are you a vegetarian now?" he pressed.

"I have no idea, Corey," she whispered harshly. "Leave me alone about it, okay?"

He made a dramatic cringing gesture, as though he expected her to attack him at any moment. Then he put his arm around her shoulders and squeezed hard. "Sorry," he said.

Ginny felt a thrill go down her spine. For a moment she just sat there, frozen, feeling his warm hand on her arm, her shoulder pressed into his chest. Holy moly! she thought. Freeze-frame, stop the motion!

He patted her arm sweetly, then released her. After that they didn't say a single word.

Ginny had been waiting for the perfect moment to bring out her tarts, about the time when the meal was winding down but people hadn't yet started to wash up and move to the next activity. Judging that the moment had arrived,

Ginny quietly got up and went into the roundhouse.

To keep the tarts a secret, she had stored them in her sleeping cubicle. After arranging them artistically on a board, she had covered them with a clean cloth, then slipped them under her bed. She had saved a few of the plumpest blackberries to use as a garnish. She was only sorry that she couldn't slip them back into the oven for about three minutes to crisp them up.

Squatting down in the darkness, she slid the board out from its hiding place and carried it into the main room. She set it down on a basket, got her bowl of berries, and removed the cloth.

"Oh, no!" she gasped, tears rising in her eyes. She should have known! They heard rats running around in the thatch every night. Rats got into the barley and stole the eggs. Why hadn't she realized they would get into her tarts too? What a stupid, stupid hiding place!

There was not a single one left whole. The rats had gone after the pastry, nibbling around the edges and off the tops. What remained looked utterly disgusting. There were crumbs and smeared berry juice all over the board and even one or two rat droppings.

It was just too much. Ginny sank to the floor, her face in her hands, sobbing. She felt like staying there, in that position, for the rest of her life.

She heard someone walk in, but she didn't care. There was a gentle hand stroking her hair. "Oh, no!" echoed her dad.

Ginny didn't say a word. Hugh walked around her and

leaned over the ruined tarts. He studied them for a while. Then he said, "We can solve this problem."

"Yeah, right!" she said bitterly.

"No, really," he said. "I mean, if you're not too fussy about hygiene."

Ginny looked up from her spot on the floor. "They look gross," she said. "They're disgusting! Did you see the rat droppings?"

"Well, I don't think we'll want to include them," he said lightly. "Come on, Ginny. 'Faint heart ne'er won' and all that."

"Ne'er won what?" she said, taking his proffered hand and getting to her feet.

"Well, it's 'fair lady,' actually. That doesn't work in this case, but the 'faint heart' part seemed right."

Ginny looked at the mess. "How on earth can we possibly fix this?"

Hugh went over and got the big board they kneaded dough on and set it down beside the tarts. He got a knife and went to work. "Cut off the nibbled bits," he said. "The bottom crusts are fine, and so are lots of the top ones. Just give them a nice clean edge and tidy up the tops a bit, then move them to the new board."

"Won't we catch some horrible disease?"

"Oh, I doubt it," Hugh said cheerfully. "What the heck!" He gave Ginny the knife and got another one for himself.

"This hasn't exactly been your day, has it?" he said as they worked together, side by side.

"You can say that again," Ginny agreed.

The tarts now looked more like something you'd call blackberry triangles, but the evidence of rats was gone. Suddenly inspired, Ginny put a fresh berry right on the top of each one, carefully placed to hide messy spots, sort of like wearing a hat on a bad hair day. When they were all transferred to the new serving board, Hugh scrubbed off the old one. "Always hide the evidence," he said to his partner in crime.

"Sweets!" Millie cried, clapping her hands with glee.

The group crowded around the table excitedly, crowing with delight. Ginny stood with her hands clasped and her face red, receiving their congratulations. Brilliant! They said. Magnificent! Splendid! They searched their vocabularies for silly and extravagant words of praise. Daisy pushed her way through the crowd to give Ginny a dramatic hug. Even Maurice came in for a close-up with the video camera and asked Ginny to get into the picture and wave. The whole time she kept praying they wouldn't all die of the bubonic plague.

Jonas caught Ginny's eye and tilted his head questioningly. *Those aren't the tarts I saw yesterday,* his expression said. Ginny worked up an enormous grin and mouthed the words, *Don't ask.*

When it grew dark, they lit the bonfire. It was heaped high with small, dry, fast-burning wood—trimmings from log cutting and old fallen branches from the woods. It burned fiercely for a short time, then subsided with a hiss, shooting sparks out onto the grass.

Maurice and Roger packed up their gear and departed.

As the firelight faded, they all stretched out on the grass and looked up at the stars, bright and clear in the cloudless night. Their voices grew quiet and sleepy, just the soft, occasional murmur over the crackle of the dying fire.

"It's good to celebrate," Hugh said softly. "There's something in the human spirit that needs to do it."

And Ginny thought as she lay there beside her father, under the dome of stars, that the human spirit was indeed a miraculous thing. You could feel sad and afraid one moment and then, somehow, rise up through it all and feel a moment of perfect joy.

Chapter 10

THE BOX ARRIVED on August 20, by which time Ginny was frantic.

The mail delivery on the tenth had included nothing at all from her mother, only a chatty letter from Andrea. Hugh hadn't received one either, though he claimed not to be concerned. Mail traveling back and forth between Britain and the United States could be slow and unpredictable. Rena couldn't always time her letters perfectly so they would coincide with Maurice's visits to the farm.

So then what? He wouldn't be back again till the twentieth, the day before school started. Even if Maurice was to take her back to London with him that very day, it was cutting it too close. Ginny couldn't catch a plane and get home in time.

Most likely Rena had sent the tickets already but they had just arrived late. They might even be sitting on Maurice's desk back at the university, having been delivered that day, at the very time he was motoring down there.

Sometime over the next ten days he might show up and, with no warning and no chance to say proper good-byes, whisk her away. What was Rena thinking? Anybody with half a brain should know what Ginny would be going through by now.

Hugh was no help. He had slipped back into his shell, growing maddeningly quiet at times and shrugging a lot when Ginny asked questions. He claimed he didn't know any more than she did and seemed to have run out of things to say beyond "Be patient."

"Couldn't we just call and ask?" she begged. "That's not unreasonable. It isn't!"

He greeted the question with silence, a deep and troubled expression on his face.

"What about that cellular phone you were going to get out here—for safety's sake?" Her tone had an edge of sarcasm to it.

"Maurice is still looking into it," he said glumly. "It's out of my control, I'm afraid."

But he assured her that Maurice understood the situation. "He will be in touch with Rena if we don't hear soon," he said. "And he'll make a special trip out here, if necessary."

But he hadn't. Not until his regular visit on the twentieth, when he showed up with that box.

Ginny's only consolation while she waited was that it gave her time to finish the house at Still Waters. She liked to think of it as her legacy. She had even decided to show it to

Corey just before she left. She wanted him to be impressed.

The thatching had been quite an ordeal. It meant gathering dried grass and straw—lots of it—and piling it up at the site. Then it had to be divided into neat bundles and tied to the roof battens, starting at the bottom and working upward in overlapping layers. Her roof would be more like the rough-and-ready tops on the hayricks than the smooth, thick roof of the roundhouse.

She put Daisy to work arranging the stems together in neat piles, a task she did with aggravating slowness. Hoping to speed things up, Ginny had invented a straw-sorting race, but Daisy just went nuts with excitement and threw it down every which way until it all had to be done again.

"Never mind," Ginny said. "Take your time. Do it right."

Every day when they left Still Waters, Ginny wondered if it would be for the last time. Maybe the next morning she would be gone.

"You know I'll be leaving soon, don't you?" she said to Daisy.

"Why?"

"Well, because I have to go to school. And because I need to be with my mom. You have your mom and dad here, but I don't have my mom, see, and I miss her."

"I miss Nancy. She's not here," Daisy said.

Ginny realized that Daisy hadn't talked about Nancy much lately. She wondered whether Daisy was already starting to forget her lovey-dovey.

"I know," Ginny said. "But the point I was making was

that before very long you'll be back with your mom and dad all day, because I won't be here. Do you understand that?"

Daisy stopped sorting straw and looked up at Ginny. "No," she wailed. "I need you to take care of me!" She was on the verge of tears.

"That's what you have parents for, Daisy—to take care of you. They really love you a lot, you know."

Daisy pouted.

"I'll write you letters from Houston. Okay?"

That seemed to make it worse. Daisy hung her head and cried.

Ginny was used to Daisy's tears. Usually they were her way of saying, Pay attention to me! or Give me my way right now! But this was different. Now she looked defeated, hopeless, lost. Ginny got down from the roof and sat beside her.

"Believe me, Daisy, I know how you feel." Ginny wrapped her arms around the little girl and kissed the top of her head. Daisy's hair had the warm smell of just-ironed shirts. "It's confusing to love people," Ginny said. "But I think it's worth it."

The day they finished the roof, Ginny proposed a new project, one that had long been at the back of her mind.

"Daisy," she said in her best kindergarten teacher voice, "how would you like to fire your horsey?"

"Yes!" Daisy responded. She had wanted to do that from the start, but Ginny had urged her to wait, and then they had gotten distracted with the building of the house.

"But now listen a minute," Ginny said, for Daisy was dancing around in her let's-go-right-now manner. "I want to do something really cool."

That got her attention. "What?" Daisy said in an excited whisper.

"I want to fire it out here. So it will be a surprise."

Daisy seemed suspicious of this idea. Ginny had known the idea would be a hard sell, but she had her reasons. The clay pots had continued to crack, and Mark, a generally cheerful and optimistic person, was now in despair over it. Ginny had a hunch that the clay along the riverbank might solve the problem. If time ran out, well, she would just tell him about it. But it would be so perfect to put it to the test first and, if it worked, make that her parting gift to the community.

"But . . . ," Daisy sputtered. "We don't have a— thing out here."

"A kiln?"

Daisy nodded.

"Yeah, I know. But Mark said he thinks—or some pottery expert he knows thinks—that the Iron Age guys used a pit clamp and not a kiln."

Daisy wrinkled her nose. It was one of her stock expressions that she knew was cute. "What's that?" she asked.

"Well, it's a sort of fancy hole in the ground, with a fire in it. I saw my dad dig one, to make charcoal." When Daisy went on making faces, Ginny explained, "You make a fire in the pit, with the pots and the horseys and stuff in there, then cover it up."

"Okay," Daisy said lightly, shrugging her shoulders and smiling like Shirley Temple. Liz and Tom have really missed the boat, Ginny thought. This kid needs to be on TV.

Over the course of the next two days Ginny had gotten things ready. First she dug a shallow pit about two feet wide and a foot deep. She lined it with hay and carefully arranged the pots and figures in the center. Next came a layer of dry kindling and finally a tentlike covering of newly cut logs from the woodpile. They were what is known as green wood, not completely dried out and slower to burn. That was part of the recipe. She left a small opening on both sides for lighting the fire.

The day before she planned to fire the pots, Ginny had spent several hours cutting squares of grass, complete with the roots and soil—like the turves they used on the oven door. It had been a big job hacking them out of the ground with an ax, and it wasn't the sort of thing Daisy could help with. Ginny set her to gathering flints to make a cobbled walkway to the entrance to the house.

The next morning, everything ready, she fished a couple of coals out of the fire and dropped them into one of Mark's little clay vessels. This would be the crucial part, and Ginny had asked Mark about it casually, the night before, just to make sure she had it right. Like Hugh, he had taken her interest for granted and told her all she needed to know.

Mark said that once the straw was lit and the fire was going well, you were supposed to cover the whole thing with the turves, filling in any cracks with dirt. The idea was that the fire continued to burn inside the pit at a controlled temperature. Ginny was surprised that something could burn in an enclosed space like that, but she was willing to take his word for it.

All her careful planning paid off. The coals quickly ignited the fire, the turves were cut and ready, and now all she had to do was watch to make sure it didn't burn through. While she waited, she cut extra turves just in case. Sure enough, on three separate occasions she saw tiny ribbons of smoke begin to curl delicately out of the mound, signaling a break in the turf cover. Quickly she covered the spots. Then it was all over but the waiting. It would take a couple of days for the fire to burn out.

Working on these projects was good therapy. It surprised and gratified Ginny to realize just how much she loved making things and working with her hands. Maybe she would be an artist someday, like her mother.

She found it had shifted her into a new mind-set, a remarkably calm one. She scarcely thought of her mother at all now, except as the ultimate destination of her imminent departure. Instead she focused all her energy on her tasks. In the best of all possible worlds—given the current situation, of course—Maurice wouldn't arrive quite yet. Not until she was finished.

She stopped bugging Hugh about things too, though he hardly seemed to notice. Like the others, he was deep into his own set of tasks: plans for the coming harvest. The barley was almost ripe.

The experience with the rain during haymaking had taught them a lesson, and they had decided they needed more baskets for bringing the barley in. Bunny and Liz got busy weaving them while Hugh repaired and sharpened the sickles. Everyone else worked ahead at tasks like gathering wood and making repairs that they wouldn't have time for once harvest started.

They were entering a long and intense period of work, even if the weather was good, for once the barley was ripe, the oats and then the wheat would follow in quick succession. After that there were the last of the peas and beans to gather and dry for winter. The easy rhythm of the last few weeks was gone. Everyone was very intent.

More than ever before Ginny had the sense that Still Waters was her second home. Her dad and all the others lived at the main compound and had their own set of concerns. She and Daisy, like grown daughters who had moved into their own apartment, now lived out here, and she wanted to make it nice. Over the two days it took the pit clamp to cool, Ginny and Daisy laid the little walkway to the door of the roundhouse.

Gathering the flints for it had been easy. They were everywhere. In ancient times, Jonah said, when that part of England was underwater, thin channels of lava had oozed into the seabed, spreading out like the branches of a tree. It hardened and later broke into small, irregularly shaped pieces that stayed embedded in the chalk. Gradually the pieces of flint worked their way up to the surface. Because they were coated with chalk, they looked white until you cracked them open.

In the old days peasants cleared them out of the fields to make it easier to plow. They used the flints to build walls or houses or even churches; you could see them all over southern England. But when they started plowing again the next year, there were just as many flints as before. They decided that the flints must be growing in the soil, like potatoes!

Ginny thought they would make an attractive path, a kind of scaled-down version of the cobblestones on Main Street in Nantucket. She dug a shallow trench in a curving shape, and she and Daisy laid the flints in as closely together as possible. Then she sprinkled dirt over it, brushing and packing it until it filled all the gaps. Finally she poured water over it and did it again. Ginny thought the path looked really good.

It had also taken just the right amount of time. Once they finished, Ginny felt it was now safe to open the pit clamp. The mound had sunk to a shallow depression where the wood had burned away. The caved-in part felt cool to the touch.

Ginny had been too busy with the walkway to worry very much about what she would find when she opened the pit. Now she realized how important it was that this final task be successful. It had taken on a sort of magical significance. If this turned out well, other things would too.

As Ginny began pulling up the charred turves, Daisy was all smiles. The thought of failure had not even occurred to her.

"Now, they might be broken," Ginny warned. "Promise you won't make a fuss if they are?"

Daisy was noncommittal. She was not interested in such negative thinking.

All Ginny could see at first was a pitful of ashes. Raking through them with her fingers, she located one of the pots and lifted it up. Though it was burned black, it was not cracked and felt solid. "Look!" Ginny cried. She pulled out another. It was Daisy's angel, and it too was whole. Truly excited now, she began scooping them out quickly, raising a cloud of ash that made her cough.

"We did it!" Ginny crowed triumphantly.

Daisy just stood there clutching her little figures and grinning idiotically. She had never doubted it for a moment.

They took the pots down to the river to wash the ashes off, then set them out neatly on the drying rack to admire. Not a single crack, Ginny thought proudly—considerably better than Mark's track record. On the other hand, she had to admit that most of the pots weren't pretty. The clay was so full of gunk it made the surface especially rough. The color was uneven too, mostly black but with flashes of gray. The incised designs didn't show up all that well either. They hadn't cracked, though, she reminded herself. That was what really mattered.

"Daisy," Ginny said seriously, "you've been very patient, but we have just one more thing to do before you can show your statues to your mom."

"What?" said Daisy, clearly exasperated.

"Don't worry, you won't have to wait much longer. We can do it this afternoon. When we go back for lunch, I want to get a coal from the fire. That way we can have our own little campfire out here, and I can try out my pots, see if I can boil water in them over hot coals. They might not be as strong as they look, you see. But if they are, well, it will be really fun to show everybody."

"Okay," Daisy said, rolling her eyes.

"You know, we'll be heroes if we can solve the problem with the cooking pots," Ginny said. "Actually, you're the one who'll be a hero, since you found the clay."

"Okay," she said again, but she was grinning now.

They brought the pots and figurines into the compound on August 19. Just under the wire, it had seemed to Ginny, like those people you saw on TV every April 15, down at the post office with their income tax forms at a quarter to midnight.

Ginny carried her basketful of pots and laid them down beside Mark in the roundhouse, where he and Karen were cooking. Ginny tried to be very casual about it.

Mark quickly grasped the possibilities. He tried out several of them right away and was delighted by how sturdy they were. "None of them cracked when you fired them?" he asked excitedly.

Ginny admitted that they hadn't.

"In a pit clamp!" he said, shaking his head with amazement. "Out in the woods! You're really quite a kid, you know that?"

That moment was wonderful. Word of what she had done soon spread, and people kept coming over to congratulate her. Liz and Tom even made a special point of telling Ginny how thrilled they were with Daisy's little figures. And for a couple of hours, the euphoria and sense of completion kept her spirits up. Then it was like riding a roller coaster: One moment she was on top of the world; then suddenly she was headed straight down with her stomach in her throat. And that was how she stayed for the next two days, until Maurice finally came.

He drove the car right to the edge of the compound, something he had never done before. Roger opened the trunk and got out the box. From the way he carried it, Ginny could tell it was heavy.

Everybody gathered by the gate to watch, curious. Maybe, Ginny thought hopefully, it's telephone equipment.

But it wasn't. It was a box of schoolbooks, and it was for Ginny.

On top of the books was an envelope. On the front her mother had simply written "Ginny," so she had obviously given it to someone at school to include in the package. The date on the letter was August 5. The people at school had evidently felt no sense of urgency. They had taken their time to gather the books and get them in the mail. They probably sent it the slow way to save postage.

Ginny, it seemed, wasn't going anywhere. She would be

home schooled there at the farm as long as necessary. How long that was, her mother didn't know. All the sweet talk and gentle language couldn't soften the blow. This was not a summer trip. It felt like her mother had given her away.

Chapter 11

"WHERE ARE YOU headed?" asked the woman as she pulled over to the side of the road.

"London," Ginny said.

The woman looked her up and down, squinting suspiciously. "You're not running away or anything, are you?" she asked. The woman looked like a grandmother, but not the bingo-playing kind. She was slim and outdoorsy, as though she raised horses and played tennis. Ginny also thought she looked pretty sharp. Not born yesterday, as the saying went.

"No, ma'am," Ginny said. "I missed my bus."

"Well, get in then," the grandmother said, though warily. Ginny slid in quickly.

"I'm not going as far as London," the woman said as she continued on down the road, "but I can take you to the station. You can catch the train from there."

"Thanks," said Ginny. At least that would get her out of the general area. She'd probably have to catch several rides before she reached the city, though she might get lucky if she could get out of the little villages and onto a big highway.

"You know, it's really not safe for you to be out hitch-hiking, a young girl like you."

Ginny said she knew that.

"You live in London?" the woman asked, giving Ginny's clothes the once-over out of the corner of her eye.

"Just for the summer," Ginny said. "I live in the States actually. Texas."

"Texas, eh? I thought you sounded American."

"I'm spending the summer with my dad. He teaches at the university."

"Oh?" That seemed to impress the woman. But Ginny could tell she was waiting for more. What she really wanted to know was what Ginny was doing down here alone in the south of England in those really strange clothes.

"Yeah," Ginny said. "They bused us down here to be extras in a film. It's set in the Iron Age." She laughed here, for the effect. "That's why I have this weird costume on. I guess it looks pretty strange."

"A bit odd, yes. But—you don't have any shoes!"

"I had some boot things that went with the costume, but they fell apart," Ginny said. That was true, at least.

"Hmm. So they're making a film in our village?"

"No, out in the country—off the road quite a ways. And when we were finished shooting, they took forever to get all the gear packed up. So I wandered off to pick blackberries, and when I came back, they were gone. My dad's going to kill me!" Ginny was rather pleased with this story. She thought it sounded convincing.

The woman drove without speaking for a while, then turned to give Ginny a warm smile. "I'm Polly Hart," she said.

"My name is Andrea," Ginny said. "Andrea Cummings."

Ginny hung her arm out the open window, enjoying the breeze and the sense of motion. At last she was going somewhere.

The day before, only minutes after opening the box and reading the letter from her mother, Ginny had made her decision. It had been effortless, arising in her mind fully formed and wholly without fear or indecision. The only hard part had been the waiting.

Ginny knew that if she left right then, while Maurice was still at the farm, they could go after her in the car. It would be better to wait till the following morning. With a good cover story to account for her being gone all day, it might be well after dinnertime before she was missed. Even then they'd probably search the nearby vicinity first. Since they had no car and no telephone, Ginny figured she had a good twenty-four hours before they would be breathing down her neck. With any luck, she'd be flying over the Atlantic by then.

For Ginny's plan to work, she had to free herself of Daisy for the day. Ginny worked out a good story but felt uncomfortable about it. It seemed so dishonest. On the other hand, what else could she do? Five-year-olds don't keep secrets.

Ginny took Daisy to Still Waters that day, as usual. For the first time in weeks there was nothing they needed to do. They just fooled around for a while. Ginny shampooed her hair with river clay, then went in the water to rinse it out really well. If she was going out into civilization, she had enough problems already with the clothes. At least she ought to be clean.

When she finished bathing, she let Daisy come in for another swimming lesson. By now Ginny felt pretty certain that Daisy was water-safe, and that was reassuring. In Houston every summer brought horrific news stories about toddlers who fell into their backyard pools. It had made Ginny very attuned to the danger the river presented. She had developed a nagging fear that someday Daisy would come out here alone, as she had before. And if she did— well, it would be a good thing if she knew how to swim.

"Daisy," Ginny said as they floated like mermaids in the cool water, "tomorrow I need the whole day to myself."

"Why?" Daisy's voice sounded mildly annoyed, nothing more.

"You saw all those books that came?" Ginny said. "Well, they're for my school lessons. I'll be doing my school out here for a while."

"So you're not going to leave?" Daisy said, splashing wildly to express her joy.

"Stop it! You'll scare the fish," Ginny said. "No, not right away. But I need to go through the books and read the outline of my assignments, make a schedule. I just kind of want to get it all organized."

"Just for tomorrow?"

"Just for tomorrow." Ginny had said.

"Sorry—but do you have any money?" the woman asked. Then, suddenly horrified that Ginny might misconstrue her question, she quickly added, "I was thinking about your train fare, is all."

Ginny looked down in embarrassment. It must have been obvious that with no purse and no pockets she wouldn't have a place to put any money. "No, ma'am," she said. "I didn't think I'd need any on the movie set." Ginny was getting into her role. She half believed it all now, about the bus and the movie. It was one of the most creative lies she had ever told.

Mrs. Hart shook her head in dismay. "I'll have to buy your ticket, then, won't I, dear?"

"Oh, no, I couldn't let you do that," Ginny protested.

"Nonsense," said the woman. "How else will you get to London? Besides, it isn't much."

Ginny thought it over for a minute. "Well, listen. What if you give me your name and address? Then I can pay you back."

"You don't need to do that, really."

"Please! Otherwise I'd feel awful!"

At the train station Mrs. Hart wrote out her name and

address on a slip of paper. She added her telephone number at the bottom. "Now, you call me if you need help," she said, locking eyes with Ginny in a probing gaze.

Ginny looked down in embarrassment. "I will," she said, folding the paper carefully several times so that it fit easily in her hand.

When Mrs. Hart had bought the ticket, she took Ginny's arm and led her over to a bench. They both sat down. "How do you plan to get to your house from the station?" Mrs. Hart asked.

"I'll walk. It's not too far."

"There are a number of different train stations in London, you know. This train goes to Victoria Station. Is that the one that's in walking distance?"

"Yes." Ginny had no idea where her father's house was in relation to Victoria Station.

"In Belgravia?"

"I'm not sure what it's called," Ginny said, with growing alarm. She wished the train would arrive and cut this interrogation short. "He lives in Warwick Square Mews," she said finally.

Mrs. Hart considered for a minute, then nodded as though satisfied. "That's in Pimlico, I think," she said. "Yes, that's not too bad a walk. Except that you don't have any shoes," she added.

Ginny shrugged. "It's not a problem. I go barefoot all the time." She was terrified the woman would take off her own shoes right then and there and give them to her. She didn't, though. She just put a sinewy hand on Ginny's arm and asked her again in a low voice, "Do you promise me you're not running away? I'd feel just dreadful if I helped a young girl do that."

"I promise," Ginny said, "I'm not running away. I'm going home."

It had disappointed Ginny that when she told Corey what she was about to do, he had not been the least surprised. "I thought you might take off when those books arrived," he said. They were walking down the path toward the forest in the long summer twilight after dinner.

"Why?" Ginny asked. "What made you think that?"

"The way you looked," he said, turning to smile at her. "Not off your head. Just really calm. Like everything was all settled."

Ginny laughed softly to herself. "That's how I felt," she said.

"So what's the big secret?" he asked. "Where are you taking me?"

"You'll see," Ginny said. "It's something I want to show you before I go. It has to do with Daisy. It's the place we go all day when I'm baby-sitting."

"Out in the woods?"

"Yeah. I found her out there that day in the rain, remember? It's off the path, hidden by some trees. The only reason I found her was because I heard her crying."

"Some kind of hiding place, is it?"

"Sort of. There was a ruined little wattle structure out there. The wild boys made it last winter—"

"The wild boys!"

"Nat and Sam. That's what I call them."

Corey laughed. "Yeah, that's about right," he said.

"So I thought she was likely to go there again some-time—when she's upset, maybe. I wouldn't be surprised if she runs out there as soon as she discovers I'm gone. Anyway, somebody needs to know where to find her."

Corey nodded.

When they reached the little clearing, Ginny gestured grandly with one hand to indicate the little house, the walk-way, the tidy yard.

"Wow!" he said, taken aback. "You said it was a ruin. That's a proper little house!"

"We fixed it up," Ginny said, enjoying the under-statement.

"You did all this?"

"Daisy helped, especially with the walls."

Corey was circling the house, studying it carefully. "Maybe I'll come out here myself sometime," he said, "if you and Daisy don't mind."

"Sure," Ginny said. "Why not?"

"Can I go inside?"

"Yeah, but watch your head." Corey got on his hands and knees and crawled inside. Ginny followed. It was cool and dark in there.

"If you brought some sheepskins out here, you could make a cozy bed," he said.

"Yeah, I thought of that, but someone would notice they were gone."

Corey lay back on the dirt floor, his arms folded behind his head. Speckles of light filtered through the holes in the thatch, like fireflies in the dark. "What do you do when you're out here?" he asked.

"Most of the time we've been working," she said. "We just finished it two days ago. But there's the river for swimming, and there's blackberries too."

Corey's breathing grew slow and shallow, as though he had fallen asleep. Ginny hugged her knees and took in the sense of him so close beside her. As though she had stumbled on a fawn in the woods, she held her breath and didn't move, afraid to spoil the moment.

Then, suddenly, an idea jumped into her mind. It made her gasp with pleasure. "Corey," she said urgently, "want to come with me?"

He snorted. "I'd like that," he said. "That would be great. But you see, I can't."

"Why? Because it would upset your sister."

"Yeah, that's part of it," he said. He seemed reluctant to say any more.

Ginny felt her face grow hot with shame. "That's okay," she said. "Never mind."

Corey sat up and rested his head and arms against his knees. He let out a big sigh. "Do you know your way around London?" he asked. He was changing the subject.

"Not really," she answered. "I know the area around my dad's flat, sort of. I spent a week there a few years ago. And I know the address, so if I get lost, I can ask directions. It's near Buckingham Palace Road."

"Posh!" said Corey, impressed. "Yeah, your dad would live in a place like that."

"It's not fancy at all. Pretty small, really."

Corey made a mildly disbelieving noise. "Look," he said, "let me give you Mia's number. Just in case you get stuck—you know what I mean?"

"Your girlfriend?" Ginny asked.

"Yeah. She's very sharp, Mia. Knows her way around." Then he grinned. "You can tell her you're the one with the beautiful eyes."

"Sure, okay," Ginny had said. "Give me her number. There's paper and pencils in that box of school stuff. You can write it down for me."

After a while he said, "I'm going to miss you."

Then come with me, she thought.

"Yeah, me too. I'll miss you—my guardian angel."

There followed a long pause in which nobody said anything and Ginny just sat there feeling foolish and awkward.

"Look, Ginny—I can't go back, see, because if I do, I'll end up in jail."

"What?" she said, a little too loudly.

"I sort of got in trouble. I stole a car, okay?" He sounded angry, as though she had gotten this information out of him by means of torture.

"So you're hiding out here?"

Corey laughed. "No, nothing so dramatic as all that. Faith got the judge to let me come here instead of doing time—you know, since it was a first offense. Hard work and privation, time to get my act together and all. He said if I stuck out the year, I could come back free and clear."

"Oh," Ginny said, stunned. "That's good anyway." Then: "Can I ask why you stole a car?"

"I was being stupid," he said. "Me and my mates, you know, having a bit of fun with this bloke we didn't like. He was totally stuck-up about his car. If he caught us walking past it too close, he'd come over and yell at us. Like he fancied we might breathe on it and spoil the shine. So we thought it would be really funny to take the car and leave it somewhere, you know, embarrassing."

"And?"

"And someone saw us and called the cops."

"Did your friends get caught too?"

"Nah, just me. I was driving. The others were following to bring me back after we dumped the car." Corey sighed then and rested his face in his hands. "So that's it," he said.

Ginny searched for something to say. "Yeah," she said finally. "I guess you're good and stuck."

"Like a bloody beached whale," he said. "Oh, and one more thing . . ."

"What?"

"Your dad doesn't know," he said, "about my *special circumstances*. He wouldn't have let me come here if he did."

"Well, don't worry. I won't tell him," Ginny said. "So now we both have our secrets, don't we?"

"Yeah, I s'pose we do," he said.

The train was hot and stuffy. Ginny sat in a corner, gazing longingly out the window at the rolling hillsides and the hazy summer sky beyond. She felt trapped, her nerves assaulted by the noise, the stale air, the crush of people, the garish colors. She fought off a growing sense of panic, wondering how much longer till she got to London.

Think positive, Ginny told herself. At least for the moment she didn't actually have to do anything. Soon she was going to have to put her plans into action, and those plans were beginning to seem a little thin. Ginny pictured herself standing barefoot in Victoria Station with nothing but an address and the vague memory of a town house with a green door. It was almost enough to make her wish for another hour on the train.

But about ten minutes later they pulled into the station. Ginny flowed with the crowd as it streamed out toward the central waiting area. And then there she was, just as she had imagined, standing barefoot in that cavernous room, surrounded by clusters of people who were milling about or gazing up at the giant board where track locations were posted. Well, she had managed to get this far. That was something. Now she had to do the next thing: She had to find her father's flat.

Chapter 12

GINNY SAT AT her father's desk flipping through the London telephone directory. She found what she was looking for and punched in the number.

"Good morning, Continental Airlines. How may I help you?"

Ginny was momentarily speechless but quickly regained her composure. "I need a ticket from London to Houston, Texas," she said. She lowered the register of her voice a bit, hoping to sound more mature.

"When will you be leaving?"

"As soon as possible."

"Well," said the operator, clicking away on her computer, "if you want a direct flight, tomorrow is the soonest I could get you out. There's a flight that leaves at nine-forty A.M. and arrives in Houston at one-fifty P.M., local time. And there's another flight that leaves at noon—"

"I'll take the first one," Ginny said.

"And when will you be returning?"

"I just want a one-way ticket," she said.

There was a moment of silence. Ginny assumed the operator was busy at her computer.

"Will you be traveling coach?"

"What?" Ginny asked. What the heck did *coach* mean?

"Coach, business class, or first?" said the operator helpfully.

"Coach," Ginny said.

"How will you be paying for the ticket?"

Ginny had known this was coming sooner or later, but it made her stomach flip all the same. In her hand was a credit card with her father's name on it.

Ginny had worried about finding her father's flat, but it hadn't been all that hard. It took no more than half an hour of wandering around barefoot and asking directions of startled pedestrians to locate 7 Warwick Square Mews.

It looked just the same as on her last visit, three years before, except that the door had been painted a different color. On either side of the entrance were planters of glazed pottery. Geraniums bloomed in them, giving the place a cheery look. Ginny remembered them being empty when she had been here before. But her real interest was not the contents of the planters but what was supposed to be taped to the bottom of the one on the left: a key to the house. Her father had shown it to her, on that long-ago visit, in case she ever locked herself out. She had counted on its still being there.

Squatting down, she tipped the planter and felt around the bottom. There was masking tape, all right, rotted and hanging off, but no key.

She tipped it a little more and peered underneath. There, lying within the neat circle of wet dirt that was the planter's footprint, lay a rusty key. She wiped it off on her skirt, slipped it in the lock, and opened the door.

Standing in her father's bedroom, Ginny tried to think where a man would put things like credit cards and money if he was going away for a long time. As she looked around the room, it surprised her to see that the bed was unmade. She would have expected him to leave everything tidy. Ginny remembered that in the hotel in Houston he had put all his stuff away in the closet and drawers, rather than just dig things out of his suitcase the way most people did.

Ginny opened the dresser drawers, dug around in the back corners and under the socks and boxer shorts, but there was nothing there except clothes. She pulled out a navy blue T-shirt and some khaki shorts and laid them on the bed.

The night table had a drawer, and there were all sorts of odd things in it, but no money and no credit cards. Ginny looked in the closet. She found a belt and some sandals and added them to her pile.

He must have worried about leaving his valuables in the bedroom; that would be too obvious. Any burglar would go straight there, looking for jewelry or money. So where else should she look? The office, maybe.

The room was even more tiny and crammed with stuff than she remembered it. There were piles of boxes, neatly stacked and labeled, plus quite a few books with no place to go. Ginny walked around the room, looking for a hiding spot. The lamp table beside the couch had no drawer; the bookcases were crammed full. She slid open the pencil drawer of the desk. There were only rulers, paper clips, pens and pencils, mailing labels, all the things you'd expect to find.

Think. Where would he hide something? At the edge of her mind, she vaguely remembered sitting on the couch in that very office and her father showing her a sort of hollow book, leather-bound, very fancy. It had a hinged lid, and Hugh had called it his secret treasure box. Treasure. *Treasure Island.* Yes!

She scurried to the bookcase and scanned the shelves for leather-bound books. She found it, low down, near the floor. Burgundy leather with *Treasure Island* on the spine in gold. She slid it out and opened it. Inside were two credit cards, some coins, a set of car keys, and paper money folded over and held by a silver clip.

Ginny felt a shudder of excitement run up her back and into her hair, making it bristle, like when she put too much Chinese mustard on her egg rolls. She sat down on the couch to catch her breath and think.

Call the airlines, she decided; that was absolutely the first thing to do.

"The ticket will be charged to Dr. Dorris's credit card," Ginny said, and read off the number. Ginny said that she was his secretary, and the ticket was for his daughter, who lived in the United States. She was just visiting for the summer. Ginny realized as she babbled on that she was talking too much. She would be more credible if she were brisker, calmer. She trapped her tongue between her teeth to stop herself from talking.

The operator took the credit card number and arranged for an electronic ticket. She gave Ginny a confirmation code and explained about the check-in procedure at the airport. Miss Dorris would need a picture ID, she said, but since she'd have her passport anyway, that would be sufficient.

Oh, my God, Ginny thought with horror. Her passport! It was with her suitcase back at the university. She felt like she had run full throttle into a concrete wall.

"May I help you with anything else?"

"No, thank you," Ginny said, and hung up.

Ginny stood in the shower shampooing her hair for the second time. The warm water cascading over her back and shoulders was heavenly. The sweet smell of the soap, the steamy air against her face felt unimaginably wonderful. It was just too bad that Hugh used a crummy brand of shampoo and had no conditioner at all.

He didn't have a hair dryer either, she noted as she toweled off. Ginny wiped the mirror and gazed at herself as she combed her hair. That was definitely more like it, she thought happily. She had a "farmer tan," and her skin was dry, but she looked basically normal. She found some hand lotion in the medicine cabinet and rubbed it on her face, then headed for the bedroom.

Ginny pulled on the khaki shorts and cinched them up with the belt. With the big, loose T-shirt over them, she thought she looked like any sloppy American kid. All she needed was a baseball cap. She slipped on the sandals, then slipped them off again. They were about three sizes too big, so she'd wait until she left to put them on.

Ginny picked up her Iron Age clothes and rolled them up in a ball. She considered throwing them in the trash but decided against it. Someone had woven these things by hand. Instead she went back into the office and tucked the bundle behind one of the boxes.

She glanced at the clock. It was two forty-five. Back at the compound no one even knew she was gone. More important, no one would have telephoned Maurice. Her strategy for getting her suitcase back depended on that. It meant getting out to the university and watching the parking lot. She knew his car, and she knew where he parked it. The minute he pulled out, she would just walk in there and spin a story. She was getting to be very good at that.

Ginny went into the kitchen, half hoping for a bag of chips—or crisps, as they called them over here—or maybe some peanuts. She opened one of the cabinets and was surprised to find it fully stocked. There was even some pasta and tomato sauce in there. That wouldn't take very long to cook, and Ginny was really hungry.

As she scanned the room for a pot to boil the pasta in, she noticed something that made her catch her breath. In the sink were a bowl, a cup, a plate, and some utensils. They had just been plopped in there, and water had been poured over them, the way you do when you don't have time to wash the dishes, so the food won't harden. A few soggy flakes of breakfast cereal floated on top of the milky water in the bowl.

Ginny opened the refrigerator. There was milk and orange juice and a box of Chinese takeout. Someone was living here!

Of course! Hugh would be gone a whole year; he would want someone to look after his things.

Ginny would have to leave right that minute, and she couldn't come back either.

She stopped to consider whether she had left any traces behind—besides stealing some stranger's clothes, that is. The shower was wet; there was nothing she could do about that. She was sure she had closed the drawers and the closet door.

Ginny hurried into the office and found an envelope. She addressed it to Mrs. Hart and slipped some money inside. Then she searched around for a stamp. She hadn't seen any in the pencil drawer, the obvious place. Then she noticed a small, decorated bowl with a lid. It looked Egyptian, with hieroglyphs painted on it. She lifted the lid and found stamps. Everything was going her way, she thought, just as the heard the key turn in the lock.

Chapter 13

GINNY SLID DOWN between the couch and the bookcase. She heard the door close and footsteps echo on the wooden floor. Something was dropped onto a table, something fairly heavy—books, maybe—and there was the jingle of keys. Then the TV went on.

Probably one of her dad's graduate students, she thought, someone like Roger. He was finished with his classes for the day and might easily stay there all afternoon and into the night. The university offices would close in a few hours, and she would have no way to get her suitcase. And as it got dark, the search for Ginny would begin. Hugh would walk out to the road and find a telephone. She didn't have time for this!

After the first half hour Ginny was too stiff and bored to be hysterical. The television droned on irritatingly. Finally she heard it being switched off with a click, and footsteps headed toward the bathroom. Ginny heard him peeing. It was amazingly loud. He thought he was alone, of course; he hadn't bothered to close the door. Would he notice how wet and steamy it was in there?

He didn't seem to. He returned to the living room and made a phone call. He had a young voice, Ginny thought. Her student theory was probably correct. He seemed to be making plans to meet someone for dinner but kept drifting off the subject.

"Yeah?" he said. "No, I don't think so." Long silence. "No, I really don't." Short silence. "Last year I did, but it doesn't matter."

This has to be the most boring conversation ever held, Ginny thought. She took the risk of peering over the arm of the couch, but all she could see was an outstretched leg. He was wearing khaki trousers and brown loafers. She was in the process of wishing she had her own loafers when it hit her. The sandals! They were still lying where she left them, right smack in the middle of the bedroom floor. He would know he hadn't put them there. He would get suspicious and start looking around.

"Want to go to that curry place? . . . No, the other one . . . Sure . . . I don't care . . . Seven-thirty? Eight?"

Oh, no—please! That was, what—four hours from now?

"Yeah, okay. See you there. Cheerio."

Ginny put her face in her hands and sighed very quietly.

It was a quarter past six when Ginny heard him run the shower. She waited about a minute to make sure he was actually in there; then she stood up carefully. Her back and legs were killing her.

In the hours she had been sitting there listening to this stranger's every move, Ginny had decided one thing. She had passed the point where she could do this by herself. She was going to need some help. Quickly retrieving her Iron Age clothes, she pulled the slip of paper with Mia's number on it out of the hem of the sleeve where she had hidden it. Then she put the clothes back behind the box and took a few cautious steps. She heard the sound of an elbow bumping the tile wall of the shower. He was definitely in there, soaping up, probably, arms flailing around as he scrubbed. Even if he discovered she was there, Ginny realized, he was in no position to run after her. It was now or never. Ginny dashed for the door, and in seconds she was outside.

At Victoria Station Ginny found a pay phone and called the number Corey had given her. He had written it neatly in a boyish hand, with rounded strokes. You could tell a kid had written it, not an adult, and that seemed odd. Corey wasn't kidlike. He had authority and experience. People are rarely what they seem, Rena had told her once. Ginny hadn't understood it then, but she was beginning to now.

"Hello?" said a woman's voice on the other end of the line. She was speaking very loudly, as if she had just learned how to use a telephone.

"May I speak to Mia, please?" Ginny said, enunciating very carefully. The woman might be a little deaf, Ginny thought.

"You want Mia?" shouted the woman.

"Yes, please!" Ginny said.

"Just a minute."

There was a bit of a wait, then: "She's coming."

Loud footsteps approached the phone. Mia must be wearing clogs or something.

"Hello?" A younger voice this time.

"Mia," Ginny said nervously, "I'm a friend of Corey's."

"Corey?" Mia said, sounding surprised.

"Yeah, I was out at the Iron Age farm where he is. He said to tell you I'm the one with the beautiful eyes."

Mia laughed hilariously.

"The thing is," Ginny went on, "he gave me your number in case I was in a jam, and I hate to ask a perfect stranger for help, but the fact is, I really need it."

"Yeah?" She sounded interested, like she was about to hear a juicy story. "That's all right," she said, "Go on."

So Ginny told her everything. Mia kept saying, "Yeah?" to nudge her along.

"So there you have it," Ginny said. "I know there's probably nothing you can do to help me, but if you have any ideas, I'd really like to hear them."

"Just let me think a minute," she said. And she really was silent for a good minute, maybe more.

"Look," she said, finally, "don't you worry. This'll be a lark. I'll meet you at the tube station by the university, okay? It may take me awhile, so just wait and I'll find you. What size shoes do you wear?"

Ginny started to protest, as she had with Mrs. Hart, but

then realized that was silly. After all, she had asked this girl for help. "Eight," she said. "I've got big feet."

"Me too," Mia said. "I'll bring you some shoes. Once you get your suitcase, you can get your own, right?"

"Right," Ginny said. "And my own clothes too. But getting the suitcase—how can we do that? I'm sure the university will be closed by the time we get there."

"We'll get in," Mia said, sounding unaccountably cheery. "Don't you worry about that." Then she hung up.

Ginny waited at the tube station for more than half an hour. She was almost sick with hunger, but she didn't dare leave her post. She kept seeing Mia everywhere. There were blond Mias and dark Mias, tall ones and petite ones. It surprised Ginny that in all the times Corey had talked about his girl-friend, he had never once said a word about her looks.

Then suddenly Ginny spotted her. Striding toward Ginny with attitude to burn was a perfect punk goddess. Her hair was purplish red and spiky; her skin, pale and beautiful. Her dress was very short and clingy, and she walked on thick clogs that added four inches to her height. As she got nearer, Ginny saw she wore a delicate gold nose ring and had seven or eight earrings running up the sides of both ears. She was carrying a shopping bag.

Mia stood there a moment, grinning and checking Ginny out. "You're just a kid!" she said finally.

"I'm thirteen," Ginny said defensively.

Mia laughed. "Startin' your life of crime early, aren't you?"

"Look, Mia," Ginny began, feeling ragged and in no mood to be teased.

"Oh, don't mind me," Mia interrupted. Fishing in her bag, she pulled out a pair of strappy black pumps. "Size eight," she said proudly. They didn't go with the shorts and baggy T-shirt look, but shoes were shoes. Ginny put them on.

"Let's go somewhere and plan this out," Mia said.

"Okay, but I'm really hungry," Ginny said. "If we're going to talk, can we do it while I eat?"

"Yeah, no problem. Follow me."

They climbed the stairs out of the tube station. It was dark by then, and the shops had their lights on, casting a warm glow out onto the sidewalk. The area was full of bars and coffee shops, obviously catering to the student trade. They went into the nearest one and slid onto the plastic seats of a booth. Ginny ordered an omelet with chips and a Coke. Mia just wanted coffee.

Then, as they waited for the food to come, Mia went over it all again methodically. She asked a lot of questions about Maurice and everything Ginny could remember about his office.

"So, are you the only one with things stored there?" Mia asked.

"No, I don't think so," Ginny said. "Not everybody is from London. Mark and Karen are from up north. Leeds, I think they said."

"Yeah, that's north."

"Well, the point is, they probably took the train to

London in regular clothes and then changed at the university or somewhere. So Maurice would have some of their things too."

"Anybody else?"

"Ian and Millie too. I'm not sure where they live, but it's not London."

"Okay, good," Mia said. "So there's your suitcase and at least one box of clothes. Does Maurice seem like the sort of chap who would keep that stuff piled up in his office for a year?"

"No," said Ginny firmly. "He said my suitcase was in storage. I'm almost positive those were his exact words."

Mia looked thoughtful for a minute. Ginny couldn't stop looking at her nose ring and heavy eye makeup. She was the strangest and most beautiful creature Ginny had ever seen.

"So they're probably locked in a cupboard somewhere," Mia said.

"Exactly."

"Good," Mia said. "That's what I came prepared for."

"What do you mean?"

The waitress brought Ginny's omelet. Ginny poured a big pool of ketchup on the side of her plate and began gorging on chips. The smell of cooking food had just about driven her around the bend. After a couple of bites Ginny remembered her table manners. She looked up to see if Mia was shocked, but she didn't seem to be.

"Well," said Mia, clearly enjoying the whole escapade, "I mean, we have a security guard to deal with, now don't we?"

"I guess we do."

Mia added a ton of sugar and milk to her coffee, took a couple of sips, then reached down and picked up the shopping bag. "I'm going to the loo," she said. "Back in a jiffy."

Ginny ate ravenously, to the point that she almost felt sick. She ordered another Coke and waited.

After about ten minutes a middle-aged woman came and sat down across from her. "What do you think?" said Mia's voice. Ginny's jaw dropped.

"A master of disguises," Mia said with obvious satisfaction. "The wig is my mum's. Not bad, eh?"

It wasn't just the wig, which was brown and cut in a conventional short, layered style. Mia had removed all her pierced hardware and put on gold clip-on earrings. She had changed her makeup to achieve a look that was plain and conservative. She wore a rayon flowered dress that hung well below her knees and a sporty jacket. They were probably her mother's too.

"Amazing," Ginny said.

"Yeah," Mia said happily.

Ginny and Mia walked into the main entrance to the university, where a security guard sat at a desk, reading a tabloid. He looked up and smiled. "May I help you?" he said.

Mia went into action, her accent changing as radically as her appearance had. "Yes," she said crisply, "Dr. Everett asked me to come pick up this young lady's suitcase, please. It's in storage in the Department of Archaeology."

"Dr. Everett?" the guard said. He had gotten that part at least.

With a touch of annoyance in her voice, Mia explained it to him carefully, as if she were speaking to a child. "Dr. Maurice Everett, head of the department. He's running a project down in the south of England, and this young lady is one of the participants. Her belongings have been in storage while she's there, but there's been an emergency regarding her mother, back in America, and she has to leave."

The guard still looked reluctant, more likely out of laziness than caution, Ginny suspected.

"I'll need to call Dr. Everett and check on that," he said. They had expected him to say this but had decided that it was unlikely that the guard would have Maurice's home number. He was probably just bluffing.

"Well, you can if you like," Mia said coolly, "but you won't get him. He's gone to the ballet." It sounded like *bal-*lay the way she said it. Very upper-crust.

"I don't know . . . ," the guard muttered.

"Look," Mia continued, getting a little frosty now, "this young lady has to be on a plane tomorrow morning at nine-forty, and if Dr. Everett has to drive out here in the middle of the night to fetch her suitcase and passport, he's going to be very, very annoyed."

Ginny wished Mia would stop referring to her as "this young lady."

The guard sighed. Further resistance was too much trouble. "And what is your name, miss?"

Mia was prepared. They had spent ten minutes on the phone, exploring the ins and outs of the university's voice mail system, and had come up with a female name associated with the Department of Archaeology. "Margaret Brookside," she said. The guard looked down a list of names and found it.

"Sign in, please," he said, pulling himself to his feet. Mia produced an illegible scrawl and followed the guard outside. They walked across the campus to the building that housed the Archaeology Department.

"Where exactly have they put this suitcase?" he asked.

"Sorry," Mia said, smiling. "Haven't got a clue."

He let them in the side entrance, and Ginny forged ahead toward Maurice's office, while Mia bent over to adjust her shoe. This too had been planned ahead of time. Since Mia was passing herself off as an employee of the department, it would look pretty strange if she didn't know where to go. Ginny stood aside while the guard unlocked Maurice's door.

"I don't think the suitcase will be in the office," Ginny said, speaking for the first time. "But we ought to check, don't you think?" The guard just grunted and flipped on the light. The suitcase wasn't there.

"A cupboard, most likely," Mia said while the guard was locking up again. He had a mass of keys that jingled importantly.

Most of the doors off the hallway had frosted glass insets and bore the names of department members. There was one solid wooden door that looked promising.

"How about that one?" Ginny said. It turned out to be a broom closet, quite small and crammed full of mops, buckets, and other cleaning equipment. Other than the bathrooms, there were no other doors in the area that weren't offices.

"What's downstairs?" Mia asked.

The guard didn't say anything, just nodded grudgingly and headed for the stairwell.

The basement was dimly lighted and depressing. There were odd bits of furniture piled up in one corner and several doors that were obviously not offices. They were bound to be storage rooms, Ginny thought hopefully. The guard opened the first one and fumbled for the light switch. They were all momentarily stunned by the mass of junk in there. Not just boxes and furniture, but a stuffed owl and animal skeletons in glass boxes.

"Time for a bit of spring cleaning, don't you think?" Mia said. "I'll bet that stuff's been here since the reign of George the Third."

The second door turned out to be the right one. There, neatly tucked into a corner, were three stacked boxes with names written on them: Potter, Munson, and Kirkland. Behind them was Ginny's little black suitcase.

"That's it," Ginny said, trying to sound calm.

The guard looked relieved. "Is that everything?" he said.

Ginny nodded. "The boxes belong to the others. I'm the only one who's leaving early."

"Righto," said the guard, and pulled the door shut with a bang. "Let's go."

"So where are you going to spend the night?" Mia asked as they strolled down the street toward the tube station. She had removed the wig and fluffed her hair out a bit. The frilly dress looked odd on her now. "You can't go back to your dad's, can you?"

"No," Ginny said, glumly.

"Want to come home with me?"

Ginny hesitated for a moment. It was tempting. She had already psyched herself up for the joys of sleeping in a real bed. But she hesitated. It wasn't just that she would be imposing on Mia's family and that she would have to tell them a whole new pack of lies. It was more that she was itchy to go. She thought maybe she should just head straight for the airport. No last-minute morning dash through rush-hour traffic, worried she'd miss her flight.

And the airport offered everything she needed—except, of course, a bed. She could get dressed in the ladies' room, and there were lots of places to eat. And a big international airport was sure to be full of people all night long, even people napping in their chairs between flights.

"Thanks, Mia," Ginny said, "but I think I'll just go to the airport now."

Mia nodded. "Yeah, you're right," she said. "That'd probably be better."

"I'll need to get a taxi," Ginny said.

"A taxi!" Mia looked horrified. "Which airport is it?"

"Gatwick."

"Take the train."

"I don't know how."

"There's nothing to know. Just go to Victoria Station. You can get one from there. Save your money."

"Really?" Ginny said gratefully. "Oh, good!"

Ginny's feet were killing her. She had done a lot of walking in Mia's strappy shoes, and though they might be as cool as all get-out, they were giving her blisters in about twelve different places. She leaned over and took them off.

"Here," she said, slipping them into Mia's bag. "Thanks." Then she fished her own loafers out of her suitcase.

"Now, listen," Mia said, taking Ginny's arm in a comradely manner, "when you get to the airport, you don't want to be sitting by yourself, see. A kid like you, alone—well, you'd be more obvious. In case anyone's looking for you."

"I see what you mean."

"So what I'd do," Mia went on, "is find a family. One with kids would be good, but even a couple about your parents' age would do. Then go sit by them. Even chat with them if you like."

"Good idea," Ginny said, nodding her head. "I'll do that."

The wheels on Ginny's little suitcase had developed a faint squeal. It was loud enough that people turned in their direction, wondering what that noise was. It was kind of embarrassing.

"So now, Ginny," Mia said abruptly, "you haven't told me a thing about that Iron Age place. What's it like? How's Corey holding up?"

"Oh," Ginny said. "Well, it's pretty rough. And dirty, you know. We had to wash our hair with clay!"

Mia howled. "Poor Corey," she said.

"There's a lot of work, physical work. And no movies or TV or anything, of course. But it's really pretty out there . . . and quiet. I've gotten so used to it that I feel kind of overloaded in the city now—everything all paved over, and the air full of fumes, and bright lights and traffic whizzing by. Also, it's more relaxed out there. No alarm clocks or schedules. You're not racing around all the time."

"So, did you like it or not?"

"I liked some of it. Yeah, I did—even though I was mad the whole time about being there. I miss the people. Living together like that, where everybody tries to help everybody out—that was great. And making all the things we used was interesting. You know, when I was drinking that Coke back at the coffee shop, I kept looking at the glass and thinking what a neat thing it was. It was so perfectly made and clear, too—you know, transparent. It seemed really cool to me— just a plain old glass I used to take for granted. And I was thinking, I wonder how you make something like this."

"So what about Corey? How's he doing?"

"Well, if you don't count that time with the bees—well, you know all about that."

Mia nodded.

"Well, besides that, he's fine. He's been doing a lot of carpentry. He's good at it actually. He helped Faith set up the big loom, which is a pretty complicated thing. He's kind of a natural craftsman, that's what Mark said."

"So Corey's a country lad now," Mia said, nodding her head with an amazed grin on her face.

"No, not really. He'd leave if he had a choice."

Mia gave a little smirk. "Know about that, do you?"

"Yeah. He told me about it right before I left."

"Corey likes to think he's tough," Mia said with a faraway look in her eyes, "but he's not."

"I know," Ginny said.

They had arrived at the tube station by then, and Mia showed her which train to take. "I'm going the other way," she said, "so it's good-bye then."

"Thanks, Mia," Ginny said. Then she added, "Corey really misses you, you know."

"Yeah, that's good."

"I can see why," Ginny added in a burst of gratitude. "You're really great."

"I try to be," said Mia, winking. Then she turned and walked away like she owned the world.

Chapter 14

Ginny was startled awake by the sound of her name being paged over the loudspeaker system. It had filtered into her consciousness while she was still asleep, and by the time she was really alert enough to pay attention, the announcement was over. Maybe it wasn't Dorris she'd heard. It could have been any name that sounded like it: Morris or Forrest, something like that.

For the past two or three hours she had been sleeping fitfully, her feet curled up beneath her and her arms and head draped over the back of the seat. Every now and then she would wake just long enough to stretch out the kinks and find a new position. Ginny was desperate to lie down, but the seats were built with fixed dividers, which made this impossible. The people who designed airports apparently thought that snoring passengers spread out on the furniture would look trashy.

When Ginny picked this row of seats, there had been a

family sitting there, but they were long gone now, and the airport was almost empty. The voices and footsteps of a few early-morning arrivers echoed hollowly in the big room. Ginny looked at her watch. It was about five-thirty—a weird time to be paging someone, she thought nervously, unless it was some kind of special situation. What if her father had tracked her down? What if he was right there at the airport looking for her?

Ginny wondered whether it was against the law to run away from one of your parents so you could go back to the other one. Could the authorities keep her from leaving the country? She was, after all, a United States citizen, and her mother had custody. Surely, then, Ginny was acting within her rights. She was doing absolutely nothing wrong—well, unless you counted credit card fraud, illegal entry, and theft.

Ginny had heard about cases where, after a bitter divorce, the parent who didn't get custody would actually kidnap the children and take them to Mexico or Australia or someplace. She wondered whether in a pinch she would have the nerve to claim that her father had done that. The thought made her stomach squirm. She pictured them hauling Hugh off to jail. She saw the hurt and confused look on his face. She felt ashamed that it had even crossed her mind.

She got to her feet. Her joints ached, and her left foot was tingling. She jogged in place for a minute to get the circulation going. Then she brushed out her dress, already wrinkled from sitting all that time in her suitcase, and now creased in several brand-new places. It was the same dress she had traveled in before, a cotton sundress in a pattern of faded flowers. She had a pale yellow cotton cardigan to go with it, but it was warm in the waiting room, so she had tied it around her waist by the sleeves. It looked kind of sporty that way and covered up some of the wrinkles.

Ginny headed for the ladies' room, which she thought was probably the best hiding place in the whole airport. She had spent a lot of time in there already.

It had been her very first stop upon arriving at the airport the night before. She had gone there to change into her normal clothes, brush her hair, and put on her watch and locket. At last, she thought then, she was herself again.

Ginny had been tempted to throw the shorts and T-shirt in the trash, but then decided against it. She ought to mail them back to their owner—that poor, unsuspecting man whose intimate life she had eavesdropped upon so rudely. She would even write him a short, apologetic note explaining exactly why she had taken his things, though she wouldn't mention that she had been hiding in the apartment, listening to his every move. No need to tell him that.

After changing, Ginny had found a food court and bought a blackberry scone and some orange juice. There were a few people sitting at the tables nearby. Remembering Mia's advice, Ginny looked them over and picked out a family with two teenage daughters and a younger son. Noticing the impressive collection of bags piled around them, she imagined they were heading off on a long trip.

Though there was an abundance of empty tables, Ginny

chose one right beside them and sat down, hoping to pass as family overflow. Smiling with some embarrassment, she asked, "All right if I sit here?"

"Sure," said the dad, making an effort to rein in their untidy pile of luggage.

"Don't worry about the bags," Ginny said. "Really."

The girls were talking and laughing in that silly and boisterous way kids get when they're really tired. From their accents Ginny could tell they were Americans, and the familiar sound of their voices was so comforting that for just a second she found herself hoping they'd be on her flight to Houston. Then she realized how ridiculous that was, since she wouldn't be taking off for another fourteen hours.

Ginny gazed out toward the corridor, where people were walking past in both directions. She saw a man in a uniform with a walkie-talkie in his hand. Airport security, maybe. She leaned toward the American family slightly, her head down as she nibbled her scone. The guard kept walking. He hadn't appeared to be searching for anyone, but all the same it made Ginny nervous. It hit her then that this was going to be a long, scary night.

She dragged out the eating of her scone as long as possible, and when the family gathered up their bags and left, she did too.

There was a book in her suitcase, but she was too edgy to concentrate on it. She found a newsstand and browsed through the magazines. Once again she made an effort to stand near others, as if she weren't alone. It felt strange and intrusive at first, but then she made a game of it: She was a secret agent, smuggling important microfilm out of the country, and the KGB was after her. She must blend in with the crowd, try not to be conspicuous.

As the night wore on, Ginny collected any number of different families. She watched the moms and dads trying to keep their restless children entertained with coloring books and electronic games. She saw them lean together to discuss ordinary things: *I'm going for a frozen yogurt. Want one?* They looked so easy and comfortable together, big, rowdy, loving units.

She caught herself fantasizing about them, imagining what it would be like to have brothers and sisters, not to mention two parents still married to each other. Then she thought, really thought, about her mother for the first time in two days. All her attention had been focused on the mechanics of getting home. Now she tried to imagine what it would be like to show up there, so unexpected. Rena would be stunned but secretly grateful when she went to answer the doorbell and found her daughter standing there. Her anger would last a microsecond. She would understand from the look on Ginny's face what she had gone through, just to be there.

And she was still thinking along these lines when she finally fell asleep.

Ginny now sat in a stall in the ladies' room, reading a magazine and trying to stay calm. By around seven she decided she had been in there long enough. Soon it would be time to check in for her flight, and she wanted to get some breakfast first. She went over to the line of sinks and washed her face and hands. As she patted them dry with a paper towel, Ginny gazed at herself in the mirror. On an impulse she pulled her hair up and back and squinted, trying to imagine a short, spiky cut in some interesting color. She tried to look dangerous. It was a failure. No, she thought with some disappointment, she could never look like Mia. Everything about her face was soft and round; her eyes were too large and doelike.

Mia, on the other hand, was angular and striking, even when disguised as a middle-aged frump. But Ginny sensed that there was more going on in Mia than her looks. The way she was different from other girls went all the way to the core. Ginny remembered seeing kids at the mall who were standing around smoking, trying to look tough and worldly. They looked silly instead, like babies playing dress-up. But not Mia. She really was tough and worldly.

Ginny returned to the food court for orange juice and another scone—the first one had been very good—and sat beside an English family with two small daughters. The youngest was about three, asleep in her mother's lap, a dingy flannel blanket clutched in her chubby hands. The child's blond curls were damp with sweat, her cheeks flushed.

With a sudden pang, Ginny thought of Daisy. Sitting barefoot on the riverbank making lopsided animals out of clay. Floating on her back in the river. Seen through a lattice of hazel wands, her hand full of daub, poised to pelt Ginny with it. Suddenly she felt inconsolably sad. She had a sister after all, she realized, and now she had left her behind. Ginny felt a yearning that was like hunger, a deep and basic need. How had that happened? It dumbfounded her. She had just been going through her days, and all the while this great affection had been creeping into her heart.

Ginny got up from the table and threw away half the scone. She felt dejected and confused, but she knew she'd better pull herself out of it. If she thought too much about things, it would paralyze her. Right now she had to keep moving forward.

Ginny hovered around the Continental check-in area for a while, waiting for someone to use the E-ticket machine. People were beginning to arrive now. They stood patiently in line, reading newspapers, pushing their bags forward a few inches every now and then.

Eventually Ginny saw a man in a suit approach the machine. He was carrying a garment bag and a briefcase— probably on a business trip, she decided. He set them down and pulled out a piece of paper and a credit card. Ginny sidled over near him and watched what he was doing. It was pretty simple. He punched in his confirmation code and verified his itinerary. "How many bags are you checking?" said the message on the screen. He pressed the number 1. "Insert your credit card," it told him, so he did.

After a few minutes the woman behind the counter called his name and attached a computer-printed luggage tag to his garment bag. She gave him a copy of his itinerary with seat assignments, then asked the usual questions. He answered that yes, he had packed his own suitcase; no, he was not carrying any package for someone unknown to him; and no, his things had not been out of his sight since he packed them. Ginny noticed that the woman asked these questions earnestly, not in the rote manner they did in the States. Well, Ginny thought, maybe Europe had more terrorists than America. They had to take those things a lot more seriously.

Nervously Ginny walked up to the E-ticket machine and did as the businessman had done. The computer did not ring bells and announce that she had purchased her ticket under false pretenses. It just printed out her itinerary.

As Ginny went through the motions of showing her passport and answering the same probing questions as the man before her had, she began to feel a touch of relief. If Hugh had followed her tracks, this is where she would find out. He would have called Continental and canceled the ticket. The woman would have said something ominous like "Would you step this way, please?" or "Wait here just one moment." But none of that happened.

She went through security, which was unusually slow and thorough, and finally arrived at a large central waiting area ringed by shops. After what seemed like hours, the gate number for the Houston flight was announced. Clutching her bag, she headed for the departure gate.

It was so close now, only a matter of minutes; then she would be on the plane, and no one could touch her. Ginny sat nervously, picking at what remained of her fingernails, listening for the boarding call. She scanned the crowd for anyone suspicious but just saw a lot of harried travelers.

Finally a pleasant English voice came over the loud-speaker and announced that they were about to begin boarding. Though the passengers were asked to keep their seats while first class passengers, families with small children, and anyone needing a little extra time went aboard in the first wave, people got up anyway. They slung their carry-ons over their shoulders, herded their kids together, and began to crowd around the gate.

Ginny considered lining up for the priority boarding—children traveling alone was one of the special categories—but decided against it. She would be more anonymous getting on with everyone else. Ginny realized suddenly that she was holding her breath. It made her feel a little light-headed. She took several deep breaths and waited.

Then there she was—handing her ticket to the agent at the gate and striding down the jetway. She had made it. Now she could worry about little things, like whether the flight was full or what movies would be showing.

She had asked for a window seat, because she liked having something to lean against while she slept. Ginny made herself comfortable with a blanket over her knees and a couple of pillows tucked in here and there. She got out her mindless magazines. Then she started praying that the middle seat would not be occupied. She hated being crammed in that close to complete strangers.

A large man sat down in the aisle seat. He had big, droopy eyes and stubble on his chin. His potbelly hung out over the waistband of his slacks, and Ginny could smell his sweat. Yuck, she thought. He breathed heavily, and Ginny knew, as sure as she was sitting there, that he would snore.

Then she thought with a touch of panic that she wasn't being sufficiently grateful to the fates who had treated her so kindly. She would take whatever they threw at her now, even screaming babies. Just so she got to Houston.

A few stragglers were still coming in, but the flight appeared not to be full. That was a relief. The middle seat would remain empty, and she could put her feet up there.

The flight attendant came up the aisle, handing out menus, earphones, and little packages containing a miniature toothbrush and toothpaste, an eye shade, and blue synthetic socks. Ginny took off her loafers and slipped the socks on, then tore the plastic off the earphones. She would listen to music till they took off.

"Excuse me." It was one of the flight attendants, and he was speaking to the man with the droopy eyes. "This man wonders whether you would mind switching seats with him so he can sit beside his daughter."

Ginny looked up. There stood Hugh, his head tilted comically and a dopey smile on his face. Her jaw dropped; he shrugged. And then—as if she had been lost for ages but just hadn't realized it, and had finally wandered into a place of warmth and safety—Ginny began to cry.

Chapter 15

WHEN RENA OPENED the door, it took a few seconds for Ginny to register the fact that the woman standing there, blinking against the strong summer glare, was her mother. Rena's face was gaunt and pale, her eyes sunken. There were blisters on her lips, and she smiled wanly as if it hurt her to do so.

Ginny took an instant dislike to the thing on Rena's head, a batik turban, to which shoulder-length fake hair was attached. Ginny knew why she had it on—Rena had lost her hair from the chemotherapy—but it looked clownish to Ginny, and besides, the hair wasn't like her mother's at all. Why couldn't she just wear a wig, like everybody else?

Ginny hugged her mother gently, half-afraid that a hearty squeeze would break bones. Rena's once-plump body was now unbelievably thin, her ribs and shoulder blades hard beneath the loose T-shirt.

"I know, darlin'," Rena said, as if she could read her mind. "I look like the wrath of God."

Hugh took her hand then and, still holding it, leaned down to give her a courtly kiss on the cheek. "I'm sorry. We didn't give you much warning," he said, as though it had been his fault.

To be precise, they had given her an hour to get used to the idea that the daughter she thought was in England, living on an Iron Age farm, was at that very minute standing by a baggage carousel at Houston Intercontinental Airport and would soon hop into a rental car and come home. Hugh had been worried about surprising her like that. It would have been a lot better to have phoned Rena from London, but by the time he figured out what Ginny was up to, it was already too late to call.

The three of them sat in awkward silence in the sunny glassed-in porch. Outside the cicadas droned steadily, a familiar summer sound that made Ginny think of swimming pools and the warm feel of sun on her back. She felt oddly formal, sitting there nervously with her silent parents. It was as though she was visiting some elderly aunt she hardly knew instead of sitting with her own mother in her own house. She ought to be flopped on the couch there, reading a book, or phoning a friend to go swimming.

Ginny wondered whether Rena was angry, or happy to see her, or what. You could never tell with Rena. She stored things up till the right moment. Then she let you have it.

The silence went on so long that Ginny was tempted to excuse herself and go call Andrea. That would probably not be the right thing to do, though. Finally Rena took pity on them and broke the silence.

"I think I must have known y'all were coming," she said. "This morning I had this dream. Ginny, you and I were getting on an airplane to go somewhere. When the plane took off, we could feel the wind in our hair, like when you ride a bicycle. And when we landed, there was this tropical paradise, like right out of Disneyland. And I turned to you with my mouth hanging open in amazement—and you looked amazed too—and both of us said it at the same time, 'It's Pom Tree Lar!'"

Ginny let out an unintended giggle, remembering. *Pom Tree Lar!*

Hugh stared politely at the tile floor. He clearly felt like an outsider in this conversation.

"When Ginny was little," Rena explained, "that was the restaurant she always wanted to go to. Only I could never figure out which one she was talking about. I thought it had to be 'palm tree' she was saying, and there was this Thai place with pictures on the wall of tropical scenes. I was pretty sure that was it, but she always said it wasn't."

"I probably didn't know either, by that point," Ginny said.

"It was always this great mystery until I saw it this morning." Rena looked suddenly wistful. "Turns out you can only get there by plane."

Ginny thought her mother was getting kind of weird. This was not the visit she had imagined at all.

"I'm not dying, Ginny," Rena said then, bluntly. She

could switch subjects so fast it gave you whiplash. "Though I realize I probably look like it!" She laughed one of those laughs that mean you're not really laughing at all. In fact, just the opposite.

"No," Ginny lied lamely, "you look okay. You always wanted to be thin."

Rena chuckled darkly. "Yes, I did. Silly me. Actually, this is a big improvement. Three weeks ago I was . . . well, never mind. It's been hard, you know?"

"So you're getting better?" Ginny asked hopefully.

There was a long pause. Then Rena said, "Yeah—they take you to the very edge, right to the edge, to kill off all the cancer cells. I'm done with that part, thank God! They've reintroduced my bone marrow cells, and now I'm starting to feel a little more human. It'll take time, though, Ginny."

"So the cancer is all gone now?" Ginny asked.

"Well, maybe" was all her mother said. She paused again, as if choosing her words very carefully. "There is the possibility of a complete recovery. At the very least, I will have bought us some time."

Ginny looked over to see how Hugh was reacting to this. He was no help; he just sat there, gazing at the floor and rubbing his hands together like Lady Macbeth.

"How big a chance?" Ginny said finally. "Doesn't the doctor know?"

"It's all just numbers, Ginny."

"Numbers mean something. Like statistics. How big a chance, Mom? Fifty-fifty?"

Rena sighed deeply, her face pained, like someone trapped with no way to run. "No," she said.

"*Not* fifty-fifty?"

"No."

"*Worse* than fifty-fifty?"

"Ginny, stop!" Rena screamed. "Stop!" Then, gripping her knees with her hands, she leaned toward Ginny and pleaded, "Please, don't ask me to set odds on my chances for life. I can't bear to think about it that way. Even if that sounds stupid, that's how it is, and I don't want to be badgered or attacked or—" She broke down and wept noisily.

Ginny got up and went over to her mother. Kneeling beside her, Ginny stroked her back gently. She would have stroked her hair, but there wasn't any. Just that terrible turban.

"I'm sorry, Mom," she said.

When everybody had calmed down, Rena sent Ginny into the kitchen to get herself a soda and bring one for her dad. Ginny wasn't at all thirsty, but she got up anyway and went to the refrigerator.

There wasn't much in there, she noticed. Some cans of that stuff old people drink to make sure they get all their vitamins. There were a couple of casseroles that didn't look like the sort of thing Rena ever made. Probably some friends had brought them over.

There were several cans of Country Time lemonade way in the back on the bottom shelf. Her favorite. Rena had bought them for Ginny back in July. They came twelve cans to a carton, and Ginny had drunk most of them in the before time, when it was just a hot, quiet, normal Houston summer. The rest had just been sitting there, untouched, ever since, waiting for her to come home and drink them. She would carry these two onto the porch now, where her mother sat looking frail and exhausted. No longer the mother who bought lemonade and organized things and made rules and conjured up fun times and handed out wise advice. This was a different mother, one who was just hanging in there.

Ginny stood in the doorway for a moment, her hands cold from the lemonade, watching Hugh and Rena. She thought they looked like a couple, and they had been a couple once. More than that, they had loved each other more than anyone else in the world. They had promised God in a church that they would stay together forever.

Ginny liked seeing them together like this, and it suddenly flashed into her mind that Hugh was just what Rena needed. He could take care of her, drive her to the hospital, pick up her medicines at the drugstore, all that. And Ginny could cook the meals. They could be a family again.

Ginny realized that this was starting to sound like a scene out of *The Parent Trap*.

"Can I cook dinner tonight?" she said suddenly. They both looked up, surprised. "I'm getting to be a really good cook now, aren't I, Dad?"

Hugh said she was.

"And you have a stove and electricity and running water and everything," Ginny added with a smile. "It'll be a snap."

At the Rice Epicurean Market, Ginny went into sensory overload. She had planned to make pasta with tomato sauce, the thing she missed most on the farm. But there were so many choices! There were three kinds of fresh tomatoes and at least twenty brands of canned ones. As for pasta, there was spaghetti, spaghettini, fettuccine, farfalle, penne, fusilli, ziti, cappellini, conchiglie, linguine, orecchiette, perciatelli, and heaven knew what else. These all came in several different brands—both domestic and imported.

And olive oil! About thirty kinds, from Italy and Spain and California, some of them flavored with peppers or basil or mushrooms.

She turned to Hugh. From his expression, she could tell he was thinking the absolute same thing. "We've come a long way in two thousand years," he said.

In the end she settled on farfalle—the pasta shaped like little bow ties—and the fresh Roma tomatoes. She got onions (choosing the yellow ones over the white), garlic (choosing the regular size over the elephant), peppers (red instead of yellow or green), and mushrooms (the regular white ones, though she could have had shiitake or portabello). It amazed Ginny that she had never realized before what a consumer paradise she lived in.

When they got back to the house, Hugh had offered to drive Rena over to the hospital for her blood transfusion.

That had sounded ominous to Ginny, but it turned out to be a regular part of her treatment. She went every three or four days.

Rena was sitting on the yellow couch in the living room, waiting for them and reading the newspaper. She had changed into a loose sundress, navy blue. She had on a different turban too, this one in a blue-and-white print and without fake hair. Ginny liked this one better.

They left, and Ginny put the groceries away. Then she got out a big pot to make the sauce in and put it on the stove. She got out a small pot and filled it with water and set it on to boil. The whole time she kept thinking how easy and convenient it all was. Just turn a knob, and out comes water. Just turn another knob, and out comes fire. A clean place to store food. A cold place to store fresh things. Milk already out of the cow. How could her perceptions have changed so much in such a short time?

When the water came to a boil, she slipped the tomatoes in, three or four at a time. After about thirty seconds she scooped them out again with a slotted spoon and put more in. Under running water (running water!) the skins slipped neatly off. She popped them open with her thumb and scooped out the seeds into the disposal (disposal!). After a while she had a bowlful of seedless, skinless tomatoes, ready to chop.

Ginny was starting to feel a little dopey. She'd only had about three hours of sleep the night before. She hoped they didn't all nod off during dinner—Ginny and Hugh because of jet lag, Rena because she was tired all the time anyway.

That night, Ginny thought joyfully, she would get to sleep in her own room in a soft bed with clean sheets. What an amazing luxury that seemed to her now.

Hugh had intended to go to a hotel, but Rena had said that was silly. They had a perfectly good guest room, and besides, she said, "it won't be for that long anyway." Ginny had been afraid to probe into that comment too far, but she was thinking about it a lot.

The sauce turned out so fragrant and beautiful, Ginny was inspired to make the dinner an event. She got out the lace tablecloth Rena used at Christmas and the silver candlesticks that had belonged to her grandmother. She used the gold-rimmed china and her great-grandmother's crystal glasses. Since she couldn't find any napkin rings, she went up to the closet where all the wrapping materials were stored and got some gold ribbon. She folded the napkins in a pretty fan shape and tied them with a big bow.

Now if she could just remember not to eat with her hands or lick the plate!

When Hugh and Rena returned from the hospital, Rena went to lie down for an hour. Hugh came into the kitchen. "Need any help?" he asked.

"No," Ginny said. "All I have to do is boil the pasta and heat up the garlic bread. And toss the salad."

"Very un-Iron Age," he said. This was clearly a compliment. "Smells great."

"Did you check out the dining room?"

Hugh peered around the corner. He stared at the table somewhat longer than necessary. Ginny wondered whether the forks were in the wrong place.

"Wow," he said finally without a whole lot of enthusiasm.

"What's wrong?"

"Nothing's wrong, only . . ."

"Only what?"

"I just don't want you to be disappointed if your mother doesn't eat all that much."

"I don't understand why she's so sick," Ginny said. "Kristen's mom had chemotherapy and she had to wear a wig and all, but other than that, she looked pretty normal. And she went on doing regular things, going to the store, driving carpool."

"This isn't just chemotherapy, though," Hugh said.

"What is it then?"

"I told you before. A bone marrow transplant."

"Yeah, I remember that, but why should that be worse? I would think it would be better—you know, getting new bone marrow and all."

"Well, they had to completely wipe out all her bone marrow first, you see. So they use more powerful drugs than with regular chemotherapy. They hit her with it just about as hard as the body can stand, I think. I'm sorry, Ginny, I'm not a doctor. I'm not explaining this very well."

"That's okay. I sort of get it."

"So, anyway, the point I was trying to make is that I'm not sure she'll feel up to a formal dinner party just yet, and you've gone to so much trouble. . . ."

"The reason she's not hungry," Ginny said, "is that she's been living on Ensure and tuna casseroles. I'll bet you anything she'll eat this." She bent over the pot and sniffed appreciatively, to demonstrate her point.

Hugh stood there for the longest time, not speaking. Ginny could practically hear his thoughts spinning in his head, like sneakers in the dryer. Should I say this? No. Clunk! Should I say that? No. Clunk!

Finally he just smiled and said he was going upstairs to lie down.

Chapter 16

THE DINING ROOM looked beautiful. Ginny had tightly closed the wooden blinds—to make it dark enough for candles—and there was this lovely glow from the hot August sun slipping through the cord holes and around the sides of the blinds.

The candlelight reflected on the crystal glasses, the silverware, and the gold rims around the plates. Ginny felt like she was eating in some Italian palace. She only wished she had thought to put some Pavarotti on the CD player.

Hugh ate his pasta like a starving man, but Rena just pushed hers around on the plate. She kept saying how good it was, though the praise had a forced quality, like the way she'd raved about those stupid little plays Ginny and her friends were always putting on when they were little. Telling them they were practically ready for Broadway. Ginny hated to be humored. It made her feel foolish.

She noticed that her dad had momentarily stopped eating and was gazing over her shoulder with an amused look on his face. "The cow!" he exclaimed suddenly.

"I was wondering when you'd notice it," Rena said.

"How I miss it!" Hugh said with a playful grin.

"Baloney," Rena countered. "You never left off insulting it." Ginny finally realized what they were talking about—the painting that hung on the wall behind her.

"But I didn't really mean it," Hugh said. "Actually, I was quite attached to it."

"Yeah, well . . ." Ginny couldn't tell whether they were flirting or getting ready to have an argument. Maybe they didn't either.

"Mom did that when she was a kid," Ginny said.

"Yes, I know," Hugh answered.

Rena smiled, her eyes half-closed in a dreamy way. "There was this little farm in Nantucket when I was little—it's a development now—and my dad used to take me out there to paint the scenery." For some reason she reached over and patted Ginny's arm. "Oh, sweetie, I wish you'd known Pawpaw before the stroke."

Hugh was nodding his head in assent, a forlorn expression on his face. "A remarkable man," he said finally. "He's not doing too well, Ginny says."

"No," Rena agreed. "What was it Michelangelo said? 'My mind and memory have gone ahead to wait for me elsewhere'? Something like that."

They both sighed deeply. This was a bleak conversation.

"You know, he bought me this great set of watercolors—

not the cheap kind you usually buy for kids. Winsor and Newton, *in tubes*." She raised her eyebrows to emphasize the wonder of it; they were painted-on eyebrows, of course, since she didn't have any hair there either.

"He always took me seriously; that's what really gets me, looking back. Never talked down to me. I remember him going on and on about composition and negative space. I used to put the cow—or the horse or whatever I thought was the most important thing—right down in the middle of the paper with all this empty space around it. He taught me not to do that. He wouldn't let me use black for my shadows either; he made me look for the colors in everything. Like I was a college student or something."

"You were lucky to have a father like that," Hugh said.

"I was. I know that."

Ginny wondered whether they had forgotten she was in the room.

Rena put her fork down then and looked suddenly drained. "I'm sorry," she said. "All out of steam." Then, turning to Ginny: "I do so wish you hadn't seen me like this." It sounded like the end of something.

"Is that why you sent me away?" Ginny asked. She hadn't meant to say that. It just popped out.

"That's part of it," she said.

Since the subject had been raised, Ginny took a deep breath and plunged on. "Mom?"

"Yes?"

"I just have one more question."

Rena slumped noticeably.

"When you said you might 'buy us some time,' what did you mean? Days? Months? Years?"

A sick expression passed across Rena's face. Ginny thought it wasn't entirely due to her question. Rena pushed her chair back and heaved herself up to a standing position, leaning on the table for support.

"This is the last one of these questions, Ginny," she said. "The answer is years. Or so the doctor tells me. And he sure better be right." Then she turned and headed for the bathroom, her gait unsteady, her arms just slightly out from her side, as though ready to grab on to something if she started to fall.

Ginny wished Rena had gone to one of the bathrooms upstairs, where they couldn't hear her retching. Probably she hadn't thought she could make it.

Ginny turned and looked at her dad, who was glaring at her furiously. She had never seen him look like that before. "Just what, exactly, do you think you're doing?"

"Getting some answers."

"Well, you're sure as hell not helping your mother!"

"Why does everything have to be about *her*?"

"Pardon me?" His voice was unnaturally loud, and the tone sent ice through her veins. But she was pumped up with anger, and it gave her permission to say whatever was on her mind. There was quite a lot of stuff in there too, as it turned out.

"The thing everybody keeps forgetting is that I'm a kid, okay? You can take it one day at a time or whatever stupid phrase you want to come up with, because she's not your wife anymore."

"What does that have to do with anything?"

"Are you telling me that if you were still married to Mom and she was sick and you had no clue whether she was going to live or die, you wouldn't want to know? I mean, it would be your life too!"

Hugh gave the slightest, grudging nod of assent.

"And you're a grown-up. But I'm not. I'm thirteen, and my mom is the only parent I've ever known. So if something happens to her, I'm all alone in the world, see? So I have a right to know. This is my tragedy too."

There. She'd said it. She'd "put it out there where the cows could get at it," as Rena liked to say. And it sat there, like something smelly and ugly lying in the middle of the table.

"Well," said Hugh after a very long pause, "you might have said that a bit more gently, but you have a point."

He picked up his fork and inspected it, as if his next comment was inscribed on one of the tongs. "You won't be all alone, Ginny, I promise you that," he said. "No matter what happens."

The return to London was dreary. Ginny had no great mission propelling her now. Nor did she have any answers, really. She *might* be home by Christmas. Her mother *might* make a full recovery. But then again, maybe not. It would be a life lesson in accepting the unknown. That's what Rena had said, anyway, just before they left.

They had stood there on the sidewalk, sweltering in the August heat, saying their good-byes. Ginny made her mother promise—*promise!*—to call right away if anything bad happened.

"Nothing bad is going to happen," Rena assured her, but it made her cry to say it all the same. They hugged for a long time, with Rena stroking her hair.

"When I was so sick, Ginny," Rena said in a throaty voice, "so sick I didn't care anymore if I got well, I always looked at your picture. That's what kept me going. I couldn't bear to lose you."

It was like a stab in the heart. "Mom, I was so mean," Ginny said in a quavering voice. "I'm really, really sorry. I just—"

"Oh, you hush," Rena crooned. "You're not mean, not one little bit."

"It's just . . . I didn't know what was going on."

"I know. I should've told you more." She sighed hard and gave Ginny a big squeeze. "I thought I was protecting you . . . and then I just got too sick to do anything. But I'll do better, honest!"

Hugh was standing there on the sidewalk, looking awkward. Finally he walked around and got in the car. He didn't start the motor, though.

"I think you'd better go. You don't want to miss your plane."

"I wouldn't mind."

"You will mind if you have to hang around the airport for another six hours." She hugged Ginny again and laughed. "Your dad used to call this a Texas good-bye."

"What?"

"You know—standing in the front hall, with snow blowing in the open door, while you hug twelve times and keep thinking of one more thing to say." Rena took Ginny's shoulders and turned her around to face the car. "Now, you scoot. No more hugs."

Ginny got in the car and rolled down the window. "Bye, Mom," she said.

"Thanks for dropping by." Rena was still standing there on the curb, waving, when the car turned the corner.

The flight was crowded. There was no hope of stretching out to sleep. And for Ginny, the novelty of watching movies in an airplane had definitely worn off. The earphones were uncomfortable, the sound was bad, and you couldn't see all that well either.

Hugh seemed able to sleep anywhere, anytime. Ginny found this secretly annoying. She wished he was fidgety and uncomfortable too, so they could complain about it together, so he could keep her company.

Ginny was playing her alphabet game (places: Arkansas, Bolivia, Chile, Delaware, England . . .) when suddenly she remembered something.

"Dad," she said.

Hugh opened his eyes. "What?"

"Are we going back to the farm?"

"Well, yes," he said.

"I just wondered. I mean, you just walked out on the project like that. I wasn't sure whether Maurice would be mad or not."

"Mad? Oh, he was very mad."

"But he didn't fire you or anything?"

Hugh chuckled. "Not definitively."

"What does that mean."

"It means he made a lot of threats he won't carry out."

"But he did threaten to fire you?"

"Of course he did."

"So how do you know he won't?" Ginny suddenly saw with sickening clarity that everything she had done had brought consequences to others: her mom and dad, Maurice, and everyone on the project, even Daisy. That was the problem with being connected. When you went over the edge, you took other people with you.

"Maurice won't fire me, because he needs me too much," Hugh said. "The project is up and running, and someone needs to be there to observe it from a professional angle."

"Who's there now? Maurice?"

"You're joking, of course."

She wasn't, so she made a just-shoot-me face.

"No, he sent Roger."

Ginny pictured him in Iron Age clothes. She wondered whether Maurice would let him wear his glasses. Definitely not authentic, but he wouldn't be able to observe much from a professional angle—or any other angle—without them. That made her wonder what nearsighted people had done back before glasses were invented.

"It's pretty unfortunate," Hugh was saying, "since he's not all that experienced and the harvest is an important event."

Harvest. It would be in full swing by now. How strange to return to an Iron Age mind-set, after spending time in the modern world where food sat on shelves in such abundance and breathtaking variety. Well, she corrected herself, that was true in rich countries like America or England. She guessed that there were probably a whole lot of people in the world—most of them, maybe—for whom it wasn't so abundant at all. Those people had to worry about their crops because if they failed, there wouldn't be enough to eat.

It stunned Ginny that she had never made that connection before. The people she saw in the newspaper or on television, like in the Save the Children ads—the ones who were living in that scary balance with nature where one summer without enough rain could wipe out a village—that's what it had been like for everybody back in the Iron Age, and that's what they'd been playing at.

Ginny didn't know what to do with this knowledge. She turned to say something to her father, but he had closed his eyes again, so Ginny did the same—for all the good it would do, she'd probably never get to sleep—and went back to the alphabet. France, Germany, Hungary (was Hungary still a country? Better make it Honduras), Iceland, Japan...

"Dad?"

Hugh opened his eyes again, rather sleepily, and Ginny

felt just the tiniest bit guilty. "Can I ask you a question?"

"Of course."

"Well, you and Mom—you seemed to really like each other."

"Yes." He said this very slowly, warily.

Ginny bit her lower lip. How was she going to say this?

"Is there any chance . . . I mean, would you ever . . . do you think you might get back together?"

Hugh froze. "Oh, Ginny!" he said, clearly distressed. "That's all over. It really didn't work out—honestly! We gave it a good try, but it was . . . well, it was a bit of a disaster."

"But I don't see why. You seem to have fun together. Laughing all the time and stuff."

"Yes, we always could laugh together. But it just wasn't a good fit. I'm sorry, I had no idea you were thinking—"

"That's okay," Ginny said. She felt embarrassed now, but decided it was better to sound dumb and find things out than to sit in silence and worry. "You can go back to sleep," she said.

Hugh leaned back and closed his eyes. "We're friends, though, Ginny—Rena and I—if that makes you feel any better."

"It does, yeah." She closed her eyes, too, and almost drifted off. The flight attendant came down the aisle with the drinks cart. Ginny asked for a ginger ale. Hugh ordered orange juice.

"Dad?"

"Yes?" He looked at her with a little amused grin, as if

preparing himself for another off-the-wall question.

"Remember the day we got those letters from Mom and I was all upset? On Lugnasa?"

"Yes."

"And you told me that story about your aunt . . ."

"Abigail."

"Abigail. Right. So anyway, you said something about nieces and nephews."

"Yes?" He was looking a little tired and impatient now, so Ginny cut to the chase.

"Well, I never knew you had any other relatives besides Grandma Dorris—well, and Grandpa Dorris, but he died before I was born."

Hugh tilted his head in an odd way. "Really? Ginny, I have a sister and a brother and three cousins!"

"A sister and a brother? I have aunts and uncles in England that I have never even met? That I have never even heard of?"

"You do, actually," he said. He looked a little sheepish.

"And you don't think that's at all strange?"

"Well, now that you mention it, I suppose it is a little unusual."

"How could that be? I mean, this is so unbelievable!"

"Well, you know, Ginny, my family was a little different. It was what you'd call not close."

"So not close that you have never even mentioned them? Ever?"

"Look," Hugh said somewhat defensively, "to tell you the truth, I don't think my parents liked children all that much,

225

and I gather they assumed that if we didn't drown in the pond or set ourselves on fire, that was good enough. We were raised by nannies, then packed off to boarding schools at six or seven. As for my brother and sister, we didn't really play together all that much, even when we were at home. There was a pretty big difference in our ages. And then . . . I don't know . . . we all just turned out to be such different sorts of people. After Mother died, we just stopped getting together."

"This is so weird! I don't even know their names! My own aunt and uncle! And I probably have cousins too!" Then another thought struck her. "Do they even know I exist?"

"Of course they do. Frank and Sarah—*which are their names,* so now you know—even came to your christening. But well, you and your mom left the country and I wasn't all that involved myself, as you know, so I really doubt they've given you much thought in the last ten or twelve years."

"Weird!" Ginny said again. "That is so weird!"

"Ginny," said Hugh, now clearly at the edge of his patience, "remember what you said the other night—that this was your tragedy too?"

"Yes."

"Well, we all have our tragedies. Everybody you know, everybody in the world, has some little wound they carry around with them. Mine is that I grew up without love and companionship, and so I never really learned how to care for anybody properly. And because of that, I lost a very lovely wife and I almost lost my child."

"Almost."

"Yes, almost. Thank God."

They stared at each other for a minute. Then Hugh wagged his eyebrows like Groucho Marx, and Ginny sighed sweetly and leaned back in her seat. It sure was an unfathomable world, she thought. She would never, ever figure it all out.

Chapter 17

*T*HE TWENTY-FIRST of December was the longest night of the year, the winter solstice. Though the coldest days of winter still lay ahead, the gradual progression toward spring now began. From that time on the sun would rise a little earlier each day, and set a little later, until the twenty-first of June arrived. That would be the summer solstice, the longest day and shortest night of the year. Then the whole cycle would turn back again toward winter.

At the Iron Age farm, shrouded now in mist and rain, the group was about to celebrate the solstice as a substitute for Christmas. They had thrown themselves into their holiday plans with such energy that even Maurice hadn't belabored the obvious point that neither Father Solstice nor solstice presents belonged to Iron Age lore. They had drawn the line at a solstice tree, but the compound was bright with swags of holly and ivy. A sprig of mistletoe hung above the doorway to the roundhouse.

For solstice dinner, they would have roast goose with chestnut stuffing, roast beef with Yorkshire pudding, minted peas, elderberry wine, and (in the absence of any plums) dried blackberry pudding. The whole wonderful evening would end with an appearance by Father Solstice, bringing gifts and solstice cheer.

For Ginny the day was an occasion for farewells. The following morning she would be picked up early and taken directly to the airport for the noon flight to Houston. And this time she wouldn't be coming back.

Her books were already packed away in the box they had come in, now a little soggy and worse for wear. Someone from Maurice's office would repack them for her and send them back to Houston. Her suitcase was in her cubicle, too, so she could change clothes and groom herself a little before getting on the airplane.

Piled on top of the box were a few things she planned to take back with her. Chief among them was her mother's Christmas present, the finest of the pots she had made. Though small, it had a lovely shape and an unusually smooth surface for a pot made from the river clay at Still Waters. By a stroke of fool's luck, the firing had blackened the edges around the incised design, leaving the deeper recesses their natural gray. It was a stunning effect, and Ginny knew that Rena would love it.

Next to the pot, wrapped up in her spare set of Iron Age underwear, were three other presents: one for Corey, one for Daisy, and one for her dad. A fourth gift, a little leather pouch, had already been turned over to Mark for the group gift exchange.

Like everyone else in the village, she had been working on these things, off and on, since the harvest ended, almost a month before. Though threshing still went on, and the animals still needed to be looked after, and wood gathered and food prepared, the pace of work had slowed on the farm. People needed a rest; they needed their spirits lifted a bit. Solstice was just the thing.

Ginny was pleased with the gift she had made for Daisy, a miniature clay ark, complete with Noah, his wife, and a lot of little animals. Mark had fired them for her in the kiln. Then, since she had no paints with which to decorate them, she had mixed charcoal with lard and applied the color with a slender twig: stripes on the zebras and spots on the giraffes.

She had made them out at Still Waters, over a period of many days. Since Daisy had been there with her the entire time (and since Daisy had her own secret projects too), they made a pact not to look at what the other was doing. They worked with their backs to each other, and whenever they took a break, they covered their work with a cloth.

As the days had grown colder, they started bringing a coal with them each day, so they could start a fire. Ginny had found it quite cozy sitting there, backs touching, fire crackling, busy hands at work. Sometimes they even sang.

Ginny taught Daisy a few rounds, old campfire chestnuts like "Row, Row, Row Your Boat" and "Make New

Friends." Then they moved on to "Kum Ba Yah," with Ginny singing alto. That hadn't worked out too well, since Daisy kept straying off the main tune and onto Ginny's part.

"Just listen to your own voice," Ginny said. "Don't listen to me."

"I can't," Daisy answered.

"Then what if you sing really loud and I do the harmony really soft—want to try that?"

Daisy said she did but then sang at exactly the same volume as before. Ginny gave up on the fancy stuff and moved on to Christmas carols.

Now, after all the work and all the waiting, Ginny went in search of Daisy to give her the ark. It bothered Ginny a little that she had no way of wrapping it properly. A gift lost some of its mystery, she thought, if you just handed it over without the ceremony of untying ribbons, tearing paper, breaking the tape off the box with your fingernail. In the end, simply to keep the pieces from knocking against one another and chipping, she had found an old basket and filled it with straw, then arranged all the pieces in it artistically, like so many Easter eggs. It would be an easy way for Daisy to carry them around, and it looked kind of cute.

Ginny found her and indicated the basket, draped mysteriously with a dishcloth. "Merry Solstice, Daisy," she said.

Daisy's face shone. She scampered over and took the basket.

"Be careful, now. It's fragile."

Daisy lifted the cloth and gasped with joy. As soon as she saw her Noah's Ark, Daisy dropped to the ground and began taking the pieces out, arranging them, talking to them. She quickly forgot that Ginny was even there.

It was thrilling, Ginny thought, to have caused such perfect happiness. God could do that any old time—or all the time, for that matter—and she wondered why He didn't. That's what she would do, if she were God. Not stick people with terrible diseases or make them sad or lonely.

Maybe He couldn't help it, just like Ginny couldn't help the fact that Daisy would be sad when she left the next day. She wondered whether Daisy would go off into the woods and weep for her, the way she had for her lovey-dovey.

Sitting there, watching Daisy line up her procession of little animals, Ginny decided that probably Daisy would be just fine. She had a firm foundation now.

Ginny remembered what Hugh had said about his family, and she thought maybe Daisy had been rescued from a fate like that. Not that Tom and Liz hadn't always loved their daughter. They were just too self-absorbed, too busy all the time. Ginny imagined them running off to classes, sitting in the library, spending their whole days away from the house and away from each other. Maybe they would see Daisy briefly over breakfast, then give her a big squeeze before the nanny put her to bed. But living out here had changed all that.

Ginny used to think this project was artificial. The "real world" consisted of the places and lives they had all left behind. Yet now she could see that it was really more "real" being here, where you grew the food you ate and built the fire that kept you warm and where people worked together instead of leading separate, parallel lives. It had been good for Liz and Tom and Daisy. It had been good for all of them. Or that's the way Ginny saw it anyway.

Daisy looked up at her and grinned. "Thanks, Ginny," she said, then plopped herself down in Ginny's lap and kissed her.

"I have a present too," she said then. "Wait a minute." She started to run off to her room to get it but turned and paused. "Watch the animals," she said. Ginny promised she would.

After a couple of minutes Daisy returned, her hands behind her back. "Ready?"

"Yes."

"Close your eyes."

Ginny did.

There was a long silence. After about a minute Ginny figured Daisy had forgotten the fanfare, so she just opened her eyes. Sure enough, Daisy was waiting, hands out, clutching Lulu's horsey.

"For me?" cried Ginny, touched to the core.

Daisy nodded.

"But what will Lulu do without her horsey to ride around on?"

"She's got a lot of them," Daisy said. That was true. But this was the first one Daisy had made, and it was just as dopey and unhorselike and lovable as ever, and Ginny was thrilled.

"Thank you, Daisy," she said, "I will treasure it forever."

Daisy just nodded. Of course she would.

"Daisy," Ginny said, getting serious now, "you remember I'm leaving tomorrow?"

Daisy's expression changed to a pout. "Yes," she said.

"Well, you know, when I left before, I thought about you a lot."

Daisy didn't say anything, but she looked interested.

"And what I thought was—I don't have a sister, and you don't have one either."

Daisy nodded.

"Well, I was wondering if you'd like to be sort of honorary sisters—you and me."

"Hon-o-ra-ry?" Daisy looked puzzled.

"Like pretend. Or like we just decide to be sisters, even though we're not really."

"Okay!" Daisy said.

"And we'll write letters to each other and send gifts. And when I come to London to see my dad, we'll go places together, like to the movies and out for ice cream."

"Yeah!"

"And when you learn to read, I'll send you all my favorite books. And when you're older and my mom is better, we'll invite you to visit us. Maybe you can come to Nantucket. You'd like that. There's a beach."

Daisy was nodding maniacally; she was clearly going into overdrive.

Ginny held out her arms, and Daisy bounced into them.

"Okay," Ginny said. "It's settled then. Girl hug!"

* * *

Throughout the day Ginny had been watching other private Christmases take place all over the compound. Couples would stroll off by themselves, clutching packages. Then before long they'd be hugging and kissing. She knew this was because they had just exchanged their gifts, but it struck her that she didn't see them hugging and kissing at other times. Since she hadn't grown up with married parents, she didn't have much to go on, but she didn't remember seeing her friends' parents doing that sort of thing either—hugging and kissing—not the way teenagers did. She wondered if that meant that married people stopped loving each other after a while. Or whether it just turned into a different kind of love, the kind you didn't have to shout from the rooftops.

Ginny knew Corey loved her in a way. He enjoyed her company and thought she was funny. He truly cared what happened to her. And that wasn't chopped chicken liver either, being loved like that, especially by someone like Corey.

But it was different from how she felt about him. In her mind sometimes she pretended they were sweethearts. She imagined kissing him. But if she was honest with herself—and she tried to be—she knew that it was all just a fantasy. Corey was practically grown up. He had beard fuzz on his face. He had a strange but gorgeous girlfriend back in London who was his own age.

She would have to say good-bye to him in just the right way, she decided: tender and warm but still a little reserved.

Let him take the lead. That way she could her keep her dignity.

She had made a gift for him that was just right too—something very grown-up and manly. It was a woolen scarf, and it had been her own creation every step of the way.

First she had spun the wool, using a drop spindle. This had been hard at first, but now she could do it naturally, without thinking.

The next step was to dye the yarn, but dyeing—along with pottery and soapmaking—had proved to be one of the "problem crafts." The colors invariably came out pale and muddy. They had scrupulously followed the ancient recipes, steeping certain barks and plants in water, then adding the yarn along with a mordant to fix the colors. The mordant was both authentic and traditional, the same one the Romans had used. But it caused no end of jokes. It was human urine, collected in a clay pot kept in the lavatory. There was a theory that it would work better if the urine was stale. They tried it both ways, but neither was particularly effective.

With the dyeing ordeal behind her, Ginny then had to set up a simple loom before she could begin weaving. She laid out the long warp threads in stripes of two colors—an earthy yellow, from the flowers of St.-John's-wort, and an elderberry purple. Working back into them with the woof, she had used stripes of the same two colors, thus creating a simple plaid.

The concept of weaving was not hard for her to grasp—Ginny had woven her share of potholders back in kindergarten, and the principle was the same—but it took great care to weave the delicate yarn so the fabric was tight and even. Ginny didn't want the scarf to look crude and home-made, because she hoped Corey would go on wearing it even after he returned to London. That way, at least, he would think of her now and then, when he wrapped the scarf around his neck on a winter day.

Early in the afternoon Corey came into the roundhouse, where Ginny was helping Millie and Ian with the cooking.

"Hey, Ginny," he said, "have you got a minute?"

"Yeah," she said, brushing flour off her hands.

He gestured out the door with his head. "Come on. I have something to give you."

"Be right there," she said, her heart doing double time. She ran in and got his scarf, holding it behind her, so he couldn't see.

They walked to the spot at the edge of the woods where he had found her back in July, reading her mother's first letter. It was damp and cool there now, but it was still a pretty place, with a nice vista of the wintry valley stretched out before them.

Corey just sat there beside her for a while, looking quiet and pensive. Ginny figured she might as well go first.

Taking a leaf out of Daisy's book, she made him close his eyes. Then she draped the scarf around his neck "Merry Solstice!" she said.

"Look at that!" Corey said, rubbing the soft wool against his cheek. "Ginny, it's super!"

He kissed her then, just reached out with one hand to touch her hair and bent forward until she felt his cool lips on hers. It was the sort of kiss he might have given his mother, quick and sweet, but all the same, Ginny found it hard to breathe. She knew she would remember that moment for years—maybe for the rest of her life— yet she had to sit there and act cool, like she wasn't fried inside.

"Okay, now you have to close your eyes," he said, "and hold out your arm."

She felt him putting something around her wrist. "You can look now," he said.

He had given her a bracelet of braided leather strips. It was a little big for her, even tied up all the way. But her wrist would probably get larger; she was still growing. And maybe the leather would shrink some when it got wet. She vowed silently never to take it off—well, maybe when she got married she would.

"Thanks, Corey," she said. Ginny simply didn't have the courage to kiss him back. Touching his hand was all she could manage.

"You're welcome," he answered, then leaned contentedly against a tree, his scarf wrapped snugly around his neck.

"Lucky Ginny," he said wistfully. "You get to have a proper Christmas."

"Yeah," she said. "I'll be glad to get home. But holidays are always a little disappointing at my house."

"Oh?"

"Yeah. Just me and my mom and my grandfather, and he

doesn't add much. He's had a stroke, so he pretty much sits around."

"No dancing on the tabletops then?"

"Hardly. We just open some presents and listen to music and that's about it. My mom has never once cooked a turkey—too much food for three people. So she has duck or goose or something."

"Sounds good to me. We have too many people and terrible food."

"Oh, I'll bet the food's not terrible."

"Everybody brings a covered dish, that sort of thing. Believe me, it's not that great."

"You know, when I was younger," Ginny said, "I used to go over to my friend Andrea's house around eleven o'clock on Christmas morning to show her my new bike or skates or whatever. And then I'd just sort of hang around. They had a big family like yours, and there were always relatives in from out of town—all different ages, you know?—and there was always something going on. I guess I didn't really go over there to show her my stuff. I just wanted to be part of a holiday crowd."

Corey nodded as if he understood. "I can't imagine having Christmas with just my mum. She's not all that cheerful a person, to tell you the truth. But when you get the Donnelleys all together, it's a riot."

"Sounds fun."

"I s'pose it is."

"You want to hear something? Speaking of families?"

"Go ahead."

"I found out on my way back here from Houston that I have an aunt and uncle."

"What, you never knew that?"

"No, my dad forgot to mention it."

Corey exploded with laughter, leaning forward to beat his fists on the ground to point up the hilarity.

"Well, it's not all that funny," Ginny said, somewhat miffed.

"Yeah, it is."

Ginny just shook her head in wonder. "Isn't it a weird world?"

"Most definitely weird."

After a while Corey reached over and gave Ginny a hug. "Lord, I'm going to miss you," he said, with feeling.

"Me too," Ginny said, leaning her head on his shoulder.

Hugh came up the path from the pasture in the late afternoon. He'd been out there checking on the sheep and repairing part of the fence that was threatening to come down. He arrived just in time to wash up for dinner.

It had been decided that they would eat early. That way they could take all the time they wanted to enjoy the food and be festive and still get everything washed up before it got dark. Ginny thought there was something kind of eerie and depressing about the way night came so early now.

The feast turned out to be very good, by Iron Age standards, and the villagers soon grew quite cheerful over the elderberry wine. They drank toast after toast to anything they could think of: the cooks, the season, Maurice (who had not chosen to attend, on the ground that the celebration wasn't authentic and was therefore of no scientific interest). They drank to Roger, the Iron Age, kith and kin far from home, their mothers, their fathers, their pets, sailors at sea, and Doris, the aged cow, who had given her life so that they could have roast beef.

When they had eaten every morsel and toasted every toast, the villagers cleared everything away and got ready for Father Solstice. Mark had been chosen to play the part. Though he lacked a red suit and a potbelly, he did have a beard, a crown of holly, and the theatrical flair the role demanded.

"Okay, everybody," he announced, "outside for just a little while." He made shooing motions with his hands.

"Why?" asked Sam, who had been enjoying his comfortable place by the fire.

"Because," said Mark, leaning down nose to nose with him, "we have a surprise for you, but it takes a little arranging."

Sam still looked reluctant.

"Just go," said his brother, giving him a push.

Though it was probably not much past five o'clock, it had already grown dark. A damp mist had settled in the air.

"Come on, Mark," Millie said after a couple of minutes, "it's cold out here."

"Oh, grumble, grumble," said Mark. He stood with his arms folded across his chest, guarding the door. "All good things come to those who wait."

"It better be good," said Nat.

Even Flora gave a pitiful whine.

"Wimps! The whole lot of you," said Mark with feigned disgust. "What kind of Iron Age peasants can't take a little damp air?"

"What kind of Santa would leave us out here to catch our deaths, you twit?" said Ian irritably.

"Oh, put a sock in it, Ian!" said Father Solstice. Then he added, "Ho-ho-ho!"

At that opportune moment Karen peeked out of the roundhouse and beckoned them in.

The whole crowd scrambled for the door at the same time, causing a bit of a traffic jam, but eventually they all made it inside. There they stopped, right by the doorway, and grinned with delight. All around the perimeter Karen had placed small clay lamps, so the dark recesses of the great room now twinkled with lights. They shimmered with the slightest movement of the air, changing the roundhouse into something mysterious, like a grotto or a chapel. It made Ginny want to be absolutely quiet in there, not to disturb the magic.

Everyone else seemed to feel that way too. They stood transfixed until Father Solstice urged them to take their seats—or rather their sheepskins—for the sharing of the gifts.

Mark now began to pace slowly around the fire circle, holding a large, cloth-covered basket in his arms. Many strings dangled around the edge. Two of them were marked by knots at the end, Ginny noticed. Obviously, the gift exchange would not be entirely random, at least not for everybody.

Mark circled the perimeter slowly several times, making Santa sounds and trying to be funny. For once Ginny wished he wouldn't. She just wanted to sit there quietly and look at the lights or maybe sing Christmas carols. But Mark began getting people to pick a string, and the string would pull out a present and everybody would cheer. After a while Ginny got into the swing of it. That sort of fun, when a lot of people are happy together, had a kind of magic too.

One of the knotted strings was for Daisy—Ginny could have predicted that—and the present was truly spectacular: a little bonnet of rabbit fur. Liz put it on her daughter and tied the strings under her chin. Then Daisy just sat there, utterly enchanted, reclining in her mother's arms. Every now and then she would reach up to stroke the fur. Ginny watched with quiet pleasure. The fire lit up their faces with a warm glow, Liz and Tom and Daisy. They were so beautiful, so perfect! The holy family.

The other knotted string was for Karen, and the present was obviously from Mark. It was a clay goblet, its stem remarkably slender and its shape elegant. Ginny knew how hard it was to make something like that without a potter's wheel.

"Fill it up!" everyone called, and the goblet was duly christened with elderberry wine. All smiles, Karen stood and offered a toast.

"To one and all on this solstice night, I drink to my good

friends. As Tiny Tim so wisely observed, 'God bless us every one!'"

"Hear! Hear!" they all replied.

And they did feel blessed, every one of them.

As the evening drew to a close, the little fairy lamps guttered out one by one. Like Cinderella after the ball, the roundhouse returned to its ordinary state. The magic was gone. People began to stretch and yawn and straggle off to bed.

Ginny wasn't sure what to do next. She still hadn't given Hugh his present, and he hadn't given her one either. Nor had he said anything or made any indication that they had a private Christmas yet to share.

Now, with Father Solstice sound asleep and only a few hangers-on left talking quietly by the central hearth, Ginny had to admit that the day was pretty much over. Was it possible that he had nothing for her at all?

Maybe he had planned to give it to her tomorrow, when she left—to take home and open on Christmas morning. Or maybe he thought it didn't really matter when he gave it to her. Suddenly Ginny felt really irritated. She wanted to do it now. She got to her feet, and headed for their cubicle, where Hugh's present was hidden.

She had knitted him a stocking cap in the same soft yellow as Corey's scarf, with a stripe around the middle in blackberry gray. Karen had taught her how to knit and rescued her from an endless series of dropped stitches, assuring her constantly that it was a lot easier with proper knitting needles. But by then Ginny had already decided that knitting really wasn't her thing, though she did think the hat looked pretty good. It reminded her of one her mother had bought in Nantucket. The salesgirl had said it was handmade, evidently something in its favor. Well, Ginny's hat was handmade too; it was even hand-spun and hand-dyed!

She was glad it had turned out so nice. He'd feel really, really guilty when he got it. Ginny felt a big sulk coming on.

"Ginny, wait," Hugh said.

She turned.

"I wanted to give you something."

"Oh," she said, "well, hold on. I was just going to fetch your present."

"Fine," he said.

Ginny found herself grinning with relief.

Returning to their little spot by the fire, she handed her offering over. Though she had not been able to come up with any substitute for wrapping paper, she had rolled up the hat and tied it with a ribbon of straw. She had gotten the idea from the way Rena sometimes wrapped gifts in recycled paper, using raffia for the bow. Sometimes she would tuck in a little dried flower. The result was beautiful in a simple, natural way. That was the look Ginny had been after.

The straw had been stiff at first, but she had soaked it in water for a little while, then wrapped it around her hand till it softened. In the end, it had become quite supple and made a nice bow. She had tucked in a sprig of holly, freshly cut so it wouldn't be all dried out.

"You just don't do anything halfway, do you?" said Hugh.

Ginny shrugged. "I wanted it to be pretty."

Hugh couldn't untie the knot, so he just slipped the ribbon of straw off the bundle instead.

"A stocking cap!" he said with an enormous smile when he had unrolled it. He put it on and turned his head from side to side, so she could see it from both the front view and the profile.

"How do I look?" he asked.

"Like a—like a woodsman or—or a champion skier," she said, suppressing a giggle. He had no idea how silly it made him look, Ginny thought. Or not silly, exactly, but not very dignified.

"Well, it's me then," he said, and, leaning down, gave her a big kiss on the forehead. "Thank you, Ginny. I actually do know how much work it took for you to make this. I will wear it forever."

"Not in the summer, though."

"No, that would be a little strange," he agreed. Then he reached into his little leather pouch and pulled out something small. "Mine's not wrapped, I'm afraid," he said.

He laid into her outstretched palm a metal amulet, which hung from a leather thong by a tiny loop. She held it closer to the light so she could see it better. It was about the size of a quarter and covered with intricate work. There were small, raised disks all around the edge and a delicate sunburst in the center. The edges of the shapes were clear and fine. Ginny couldn't understand how he could have made such a thing with those whopping great blacksmith tools.

"How—how?" she stammered in amazement.

Hugh grinned. He was just dying to tell her! "I used the lost wax method," he said.

"I've heard of that," Ginny said. "It was some ancient technique. But I thought the secret was lost, like how they built the pyramids."

Hugh laughed. "No, it's the wax that gets lost, Ginny. See, you carve something out of wax, like your amulet there. The wax is soft and smooth, so you can get very fine details. Then you make a clay mold of it, leaving a small hole on one side for pouring. When you fire the mold, the wax melts away and leaves a cavity you can fill with metal."

"Oh," she said. "Sweet! But how did you get it out of the mold?"

"Well, I had to break it."

"So there's just one of these? You couldn't ever make another one exactly like it?"

"No. It's one of a kind."

Ginny liked that. "It's beautiful," she said. "Really, really it is."

"I'm glad you think so," he said, with such warmth in his voice she looked up into his eyes.

"Is this the sun, here in the middle?" she asked.

"Well, it could be—if you want it to—but I meant it to be a star."

"Oh."

"Because, well, this is just a silly thought, maybe, but—have you ever looked up at the stars at night and thought of all the other people those stars are shining down on too?"

"Yes!" Ginny cried excitedly. "I've thought exactly that! And how they shone down on the pharaohs and on Shakespeare and even the cavemen."

"Well, I just thought that while you're away in Houston and I'm here in England, you might look at the stars, now and then, and think about me."

"You can hardly see the stars in Houston," Ginny said. "Too much light pollution."

"Then you'll have to look at this one," he said, touching the amulet.

"I will, Daddy," Ginny said, and threw her arms around him. They stayed hugging like that for a long time. "Dad," she said finally.

"What, Ginny?"

"I want to go look at them now!"

So Ginny and her father walked out of the roundhouse, into the misty darkness of the longest night of the year, and looked up at the stars that in a few hours would shine down on her mother—though she wouldn't be able to see them all that well—and were shining now on Daisy and Corey and even Mia, but especially on them. And out there in the universe—or at least their own little part of it—the cosmos made its subtle shift back toward spring.

Chapter 18

Hey, Ginny—

Greetings from the land of mud! We had a huge snow-storm, but now it's all melted, and the compound is a mess. Everyone is really dirty. Now, don't you wish you were here?

You'd have liked the snow. It went on for three days and made everything really beautiful and quiet. When Maurice didn't show up for his regular visit, we sort of wondered. When he didn't show up for five days, we really wondered. It turns out this was some kind of record-setting storm. Nothing like it since the '30s! The roads were closed, the power lines were down, and people all over England were stranded in their houses all cold and hungry—no way to cook their food, you see, if they had any. Of course, we were just fine, nice and warm with plenty of food right there in the store-room and a fire to cook it over.

Maurice came out all panicked once the roads were cleared. He probably thought he'd find us frozen to death or something. We had a big laugh over that. Problem? What problem?

Oh, something else cool! Mark took one of the big barrels apart so we could use the barrel staves as tobog-gans. Down the path to the hay meadow. It was great! We had to bank the curve with snow so we wouldn't fly off the path there, though. It was really super, and after the snow stopped falling, we had these really perfect clear nights, so we went sledding by moonlight. You would have loved it—definitely your kind of thing.

Let's see, what else? The rats got into the barley stack—remember? So we thought we'd better do some-thing, or the whole crop would be wrecked. We ended up having to take it apart, layer by layer. Near the bot-tom, we got to where the rats couldn't hide anymore and they came running out like crazy. Rats all over the place *and us all whacking at them with clubs. Smushed bodies everywhere! Flora caught a lot too. Gobbled them down like popcorn.*

Now for the best part. Jonas said he'd always won-dered what rat would taste like, and so he and Ian roasted a few on a spit. Really! Actually, with the head and tail and fur off, it really didn't look all that much different from other meat, only really small. (Oh, I for-got that you don't approve of meat—or has that changed, now that you're back in civilization?) Any-

way, I can now say I've eaten rat—everybody did, except Daisy and Liz—and it was kind of strong-tasting, but not bad. Just what you wanted to hear, right?

Well, I have to go. Just wanted to keep in touch, you know, and gross you out a little. (Well, somebody has to do it!) I hope your mum is doing better and you haven't forgotten us completely.

Love,
Corey

Dear Ginny,

I was glad to hear that you're doing fine and Rena is all mended. You've both been through an awful lot in the last few months. Now it's time to settle in and just be normal for a while.

Things have been fairly quiet here. We had a huge snowstorm, which apparently brought all of Britain to its knees while leaving us pretty much unscathed, since we didn't need to go anywhere and don't depend on electricity. It was rather quiet and peaceful, actually, a time for reflection and storytelling by the fire.

After the snow came rain, and the mud is really awful. But we're inside more now anyway. There's a lot of weaving and carpentry going on. Mark is trying to make some sort of stringed instrument, so perhaps we can look forward to musical evenings.

I am working on some tools, trying to see if I can duplicate the ones the blacksmith made for Maurice. So far I haven't been all that successful. His are rather handsomely made. Alas, mine are poor things. Like all arts, blacksmithing surely takes years to learn properly.

Daisy said to tell you hello and that she is going to write you a letter. Liz has been working hard with her on her ABCs. Also, Karen said to say she misses you. We all do, actually.

Corey and I are teamed up in the cooking rota again. Needless to say, everyone especially misses you at meal times. It is clear now that we should have collected and dried many more mushrooms and wild onions and the like. They're almost finished, and the food is going to be pretty bland till spring comes.

We talk a lot about how we'd do things if the project were to go on for another year. We would plant more wheat, for example, and not so many beans. We'd need more sheep and probably more goats too. It does seem a shame that just when we're all becoming more or less competent at Iron Age life, the whole thing comes to an end. It feels unnatural to work that hard at learning skills and then to abandon them. But it is an imperfect world then, isn't it?

Well, Ginny—I miss you terribly. I can't tell you how many times in a day I half turn to look for you, to tell you something. And at night I do a lot of thinking—about the past, about the future. I regret the former and plan the latter, and all the plans include you.

Lots of love,
Dad

Dear Ginny,
How are you? I am fine. I mad a snowman.

Love,
Daisy

Dear Ginny,
It's been rainy and gloomy all week. How I wish you could send me some of your warm Texas sunshine!

I was so glad to get your letter and hear all your news. I very much regret missing your play but am delighted there will be a video.

It sounds like Rena has made a remarkable recovery. The fact that she felt well enough to go back to teaching tells me that she has her energy back. She always had more than her share.

I've been working hard here. Tom and I have been busy ploughing the wheat and barley fields, to get them ready for spring planting. Yes, I know, there won't be any spring planting, but since we put in our first crop mechanically, we wanted to experience every aspect of a full year on the farm. It has taken us quite a while to train Blackie and Boots to the yoke, but they seem pretty resigned to it now and pull the plough along quite stoically. (Actually, at the risk of sounding pedantic, it isn't really a plough *we're using, but an* ard. *A plough has a mould board for turning the soil over, a refinement that the Celts had not developed; an ard is just a spike that scratches a furrow in the soil.)*

We are following the Iron Age technique of ploughing the entire field in one direction, then coming back across it again, at right angles to the first furrows, to make a crisscross pattern. We know they did it that way because archaeologists have found crisscross grooves etched into the chalk subsoil from all those years before.

Beatrice, the goat, has blessed us with two little white kids. I wish you could see them butting away at their mother's udder with their little noses, presumably to let down the milk. It is quite awesome, actually, that they should know how to do this only hours after birth, when they can barely stand and the cord is still hanging off them. Oh, Ginny, there are so many things like that I keep wishing I could show you.

My mind keeps turning to life after the Iron Age. I have asked Gwen, Maurice's secretary, to research summer drama programmes for teenagers in the London area. Does that interest you? I will be pretty busy writing up my notes from the project at the beginning of the summer, so you'll need something to do, plus it would be a chance for you to meet some other young people. (No, I'm not forgetting about Corey and Daisy—you'll see them too.)

And maybe some weekend we could drive up to meet your aunt and uncle. Who knows, maybe they've improved since last I gazed upon them.

Later in the summer I thought we might take a trip,

maybe to Greece. I would love to show you the Greek islands.

Take care, my dear. I miss you!

Love,
Dad

Dear Ginny,

Well, I can't believe it—three weeks and we're out of here. And you want to hear something weird? It's kind of scary—you know? Like, I don't really want to go. I've got kind of used to living out here. Ever think you'd hear me say that?

It'll be good to see Mia and all, only there's this other thing—I've got to find a job. Mark says I ought to be a carpenter, and if I come to live in Leeds, he'll give me work. Only, you know, I don't really want to live in Leeds. It's an idea, though—carpentry. I like working with wood, and I've learned some stuff here. We'll see. I think I'll ask Mark how he got started, if he did an apprenticeship or what.

I told Mia what you said about your mum and her hair growing back—how you told her she ought to spike it and dye it purple so she'd look really cool. Mia says to tell you that her hair is not *purple. She didn't say what color we're supposed to call it, though. Mia color, maybe. Also, she said to tell you hi.*

The other day I took Daisy out to your place in the woods, just to see how it's holding up. I thought you'd like to know it looks good. The house wasn't hurt by the storm, and it maybe even looks a little better because there's grass and weeds growing over some of the muddy spots where you dug pits and stuff. Daisy looked around for a little bit, but then she was ready to go. I asked, didn't she want to stay and hang around a little? And she said no, because you weren't there. She really misses you, I think.

Your dad says the bloke who owns all this land is going to tear down our buildings after we leave—"let it revert to its natural state," he called it. Pretty sad, huh? But he won't know about your place. It could stay there practically forever, till it falls down anyway.

There's lots of new lambs here now, pretty sweet. Maybe I ought to be a farmer. Or a shepherd. That's it! Problem solved.

Bye for now. See you in London!

Corey

Dear Ginny,
I mad you a braclet and a pot. Ther are some lambs I named one Daisy and one Ginny because ther sisters.

Love,
Daisy

Dear Ginny,
I just got back to London yesterday, and it feels like another planet. I was surprised by the extent to which

returning to modern life overwhelmed me at first. I found I didn't want to deal with things—car insurance, taxes, working out my bank balance. It all seemed like needless complication. Not real work, like when you actually make something. Perhaps I should become a hermit. You could join me and be a hermitess.

I was the last one to leave the compound yesterday. It was strangely quiet and empty. The animals had already been removed, and we had pretty well stripped the place of all the baskets, sheepskins, pots, and things. I stood there watching the others heading off towards the bus, carrying their gear and wearing their modern clothes, and I suddenly felt as though some genie had come and cast a spell on us. As you undoubtedly know, I rarely get such quaint notions, but this one was quite distinct, and it made me feel sad.

Then I noticed that the fire was still going in the hearth; no one had wanted to put it out. That struck me as consoling, somehow—watching that thin stream of smoke rising up out of the roundhouse. Something of us still remained, at least for a little while.

Saying good-bye to the group was hard. Though I know we'll all see one another again, especially those of us who live here in London—still, it will be strange not to have them all hanging around the periphery of my daily life. We were like a family, really. There's the intimacy, the sharing of a common space, the being at home together, the striving for collective goals. They were good

257

for me, I think. I suppose you take your family wherever you can find it.

But the real miracle worker was you, Ginny. You are a gift I didn't deserve, and one for which I will evermore be grateful.

See you soon!

Love,
Dad

Author's Note

In 1976 a producer for the British Broadcasting Corporation, John Percival, came up with an innovative idea for a television miniseries. He wanted to build a small replica of an Iron Age farm and invite a group of volunteers—preferably young couples with children—to live in it for a year. Mr. Percival and his film crew would visit the site regularly, but otherwise the group would be cut off from all modern civilization. They would eat Iron Age food cooked by Iron Age methods, would be provided with ancient breeds of animals, such as Soay sheep, would use tools that were replicas of Iron Age museum pieces, and, in as many ways as possible, live authentically as their Celtic forebears did two thousand years before.

Percival took out an advertisement in the *Times* of London, seeking volunteers for this unusual project, and received nearly two thousand applications. By the early spring of 1977 he had narrowed them down to a picked group of fifteen hardy souls, six couples and three small boys, and they had begun building the farm in an isolated location in southern England. By May 1 they were ready to "go Iron Age"—move out of their tents and into the roundhouse, putting aside their modern clothes for homespun garments in the style of the ancient Celts.

Anxious to make the farm and its way of life as authentic as possible, Percival consulted many experts, from blacksmiths to zoologists. He was especially fortunate in receiving the advice and assistance of Dr. Peter Reynolds, the director of the Butser Ancient Farm Project in East Meon, Hampshire, who has made it his life's work to study farming in the Iron Age. At the Butser Farm, Reynolds had built a number of roundhouses, based on posthole patterns from Iron Age sites, and furnished them with querns, looms, and other Iron Age implements. In the nearby fields he planted ancient strains of wheat to study yields of grain without the use of modern fertilizers. His animals, such as the Soay sheep and Dexter cattle, were as close to ancient breeds as possible. The farm is open to scholars and school groups—anyone, in fact, who hopes to learn about daily life in the Iron Age. It is also a model of experimental archaeology. Dr. Reynolds was therefore of immeasurable help to Percival in setting up the Iron Age farm for his project as accurately as possible.

The result of all this labor and planning was a twelve-part series, *Living in the Past,* first broadcast in Britain over a period of three months in the spring of 1978. The project drew considerable attention at the time and was written up in the *New York Times* and *Smithsonian Magazine,* where my mother, Fay Grissom Stanley, read about it. She was an author of several mystery novels and was always trolling for book ideas. She had become newly aware of the children's book field because I published my first picture book that year, and it occurred to her that the Iron Age farm would make a fascinating setting for a novel for young readers. So she tracked down John Percival via the BBC and began a correspondence that was to continue, off and on, for more than ten years.

In the summer of 1983 she traveled to England to meet with Percival and to visit Peter Reynolds at the Butser Farm. She came home with a bundle of wool from a Soay sheep, a simple wood and clay spindle, lots of photos of round-houses and wattle fences and oatmeal-colored sheep, and masses of books and brochures. But she never wrote the book.

After her death in 1990 I found a file of her correspondence with John Percival and a box of research materials on the Iron Age project. It occurred to me that since she had not been able to write the story, perhaps I should.

It took me another eight years to find the time to work on it, but in the spring of 1998, together with my husband, Peter, I retraced Mother's steps, visiting the Butser Farm (though Peter Reynolds was out of town) and viewing the tapes of *Living in the Past* at the BBC archives. The book I eventually wrote is probably quite different from the one my mother envisioned, but I think she would have been pleased.

I would like to acknowledge the tremendous debt I owe to John Percival. The setting is, of course, his original conception. His book *Living in the Past,* which documents the project, was my primary source. But it is important to stress that mine is a work of fiction, and I have changed many things from the way they actually occurred. I have made the Iron Age Farm a university research project rather than a setting for a television documentary, for example, and none of the characters is based on the original participants.

But other details were retained because they were so wonderful: the breaking pots, the swarming bees, the clay shampoo, the garlic cheese spread, the failure to make soap or start a fire, the war with the rats, the snowstorm, and the celebration of solstice instead of Christmas among them.

I am grateful to Dr. Reynolds and the Butser Ancient Farm Project for many supporting research materials and for arranging a tour of the premises. I would also like to acknowledge the book *Archaeology by Experiment,* by John Coles, and *The Celtic World,* edited by Miranda J. Green. In the cooking sections I relied heavily on *Wild Food,* by Roger Phillips, and *Food for Free,* by Richard Mabey.

Sincere thanks to Dr. Murray Bern, who helped me work out the parts of the story dealing with cancer and its treatment.

Editors seldom get the credit they deserve, so I'd especially like to offer my most profound thanks to my editor of more than twenty years, Meredith Charpentier, for her continuing faith that I actually could write a novel, despite evidence to the contrary, and for explaining to me that a setting is not a plot.

I should also confess that at the time of this writing, international E-tickets are not yet offered by Continental Airlines, as described in this book, though my travel agent seems to think they are coming soon.

Finally I would like to thank John Percival for reading this manuscript and making sure I didn't make any grievous errors. Any that remain are mine and not his.

About the Author

DIANE STANLEY was born in Abilene, Texas, into a remarkably creative and adventuresome family, notable for its strong women. Early in her career, Ms. Stanley worked as a medical illustrator and as an art director for a major publishing house. She became interested in children's books and began illustrating them when her daughters, Catherine and Tamara, were young.

Now Diane Stanley is recognized as the supremely gifted author as well as illustrator of nearly twenty books for children, including a series of picture-book biographies that have been showered with awards and honors. These include *Shaka, King of the Zulus; Bard of Avon: The Story of William Shakespeare; Charles Dickens: The Man Who Had Great Expectations; Cleopatra; Leonardo da Vinci;* and, most recently, *Joan of Arc.*

Diane Stanley lives in Houston, Texas, with her husband and frequent collaborator, Peter Vennema, and their son, John.